JESSICA JOINS THE BROWNIES

G000045548

Also by Lynda Neilands:
Tracy and the Warriors

Jessica Joins the Brownies

LYNDA NEILANDS

KINGSWAY PUBLICATIONS
EASTBOURNE

Front cover design by Vic Mitchell

ISBN 0 86065 990 9

Printed in Great Britain for
KINGSWAY PUBLICATIONS LTD
Lottbridge Drove, Eastbourne, E Sussex BN23 6NT by
Hazells Ltd, Aylesbury, Bucks.
Typeset by J&L Composition Ltd, Filey, North Yorkshire.

For
Janet and Dawn

Contents

Contents

1

Beansprout

THE OLD WOMAN outside the school gates of Laganvale Primary School looked like a chipmunk in overalls—small, plump, with wisps of snow-white hair tailing out under her cap. She wore black dungarees under a long plastic raincoat. 'Jessica! Jessica!' she was hollering at a thin dark-haired girl in the playground. 'If you're finished for the morning, you can come an' gie me a hand.'

Granny Knott! Oh no! Jessica's heart sank. Usually at this hour her grandmother was snoozing peacefully on her bunk-bed in their mobile home. But today she must have woken early. Got confused. ... If Jessica had been a beetle she could have scuttled into a crack in the playground and hidden there until the coast was clear. But she wasn't a beetle. She was a horror-stricken eight-year-old going hot and cold at the unexpected appearance of her grandmother pushing a trolley-load of fruit and vegetables ... probably about to make a show of herself in front of half the school.

It was every bit as bad as Jessica feared.

'Here's a fine thing,' the old woman cried the moment she reached the gates. 'A whole school out sporting themselves first thing in the morning. Did the master decide you'd done enough learning for the day?'

'Shhh, Granny.' Out of the corner of her eye Jessica could see Louise Witherspoon in a whispering huddle with the three Rs. 'It isn't first thing in the morning. It's half-past three in the afternoon.'

Granny Knott folded her arms across a sack of potatoes and frowned. 'Now would that be half-past three today or tomorrow?'

Burning with embarrassment, Jessica heard the titters begin.

'It's Monday, Granny. It's half-past three on Monday afternoon.'

'You're telling me there'll be no market for these until the morrow morning?' Her grand-mother directed one gnarled, grubby finger at a sackful of parsnips.

Jessica nodded dumbly.

'Give us an apple then, Beanie,' a voice called behind them.

'Yeah, Beanie. Give us an apple . . . give us an apple . . .' The chorus grew.

Mrs Knott pulled herself up to her full chipmunk height. 'I'll give yous apples where it hurts,' she bellowed. 'And quit you standing there with your two arms the one length,' she turned on her granddaughter as if the whole situation was somehow Jessica's fault. 'It'll take some shifting til get these back home.'

Still without speaking, Jessica went over to the trolley and held out her arms. Granny piled them high with cucumbers. Then, side by side, they started up the street.

A group of older boys from her brother Robin's school were lounging around the bus stop. Fortunately Robin wasn't there to make things worse.

'Watch you don't lose yer marrows, Beansprout,' someone shouted as they passed.

Beansprout! The girls behind tittered louder than ever at the name. No one could have come up with one which suited old Beanie's pale skinny granddaughter better. And in the split-second that she heard it, Jessica knew it would stick. Tomorrow they would all be at it. Louise and Rachel and Rosie and Ruth. All calling her Beansprout. . . .

Tears sprang to her eyes, blinding her to the black base-ball boot stuck out in her path. Next thing she was tripping, falling to the ground, shooting cucumbers in all directions.

'Pick yourself up, girl.' Granny Knott sprang to the rescue of a couple of prize specimens rolling towards the gutter.

Jessica picked herself up and ran.

'Jessica! Jessica! You wait for me.' Her grand-mother's street-hawker's call followed her up the street.

Jessica ignored her, running on and on, past the church and the rectory, past the bicycle shop and the green grocer's. . . . on and on, further and further, like a small hunted animal speeding across the earth—to safety.

Isabel Lovett, looking out through the rectory window, saw her go.

Impulsively she called her daughter over. 'Who's that?' she asked.

Sharon Lovett had been off school that day with a cold. 'That's Jessica Bott,' she replied through a very blocked nose. 'Her Gradmober's the fuddy old vegetable-woman you see in the barket. She lives with her id a bobile hobe, behind Witherspood's Service Station.'

As usual Mrs Lovett found herself marvelling at the ease with which her daughter got to grips with a new situation. The family had only moved to Laganvale two months ago, and yet already Sharon seemed acquainted with half the town.

'Whyever do you think she was running like that?'

Sharon shrugged. 'Who dows? They're all a bit mad. Graddy Bott is doting, Robid—that's her brother—slouches around looking like he's half a brain. The girls say Jessica spends all her

12

spare time climbing trees. Her parents were killed in a road accident.'

'Poor child.' Her mother looked thoughtful.

'I know whad you're thinking . . .'

'Well . . .' The woman smiled hopefully. 'It *might* work. Are you willing to help?'

'No harm id trying.' Sharon blew her nose.

'Right then.' Mrs Lovett went into the hallway and put on her coat. 'I'll go round straight away and ask her. She lives behind Witherspoon's Service Station you say . . .'

Jessica, at that moment, was hidden in an oak tree, living in the world of her favourite daydream. The general story-line was always the same: Granny Knott wasn't her real grand-mother. And her parents weren't dead. For eight years they had been travelling the country searching for their lost child. And now, at long last, they had found her and she was going to live with them in a gleaming white house with six bedrooms, and four bathrooms, and a swimming-pool. And her own bedroom would be painted the softest pink, like the inside of a sea-shell, and the wardrobes would be full of beautiful new clothes, all exactly her size. Sometimes Jessica imagined herself driving off with her mummy to pick the clothes, and sometimes they were already there when she arrived. And sometimes she explained about Granny Knott's confusion, so she wouldn't be

13

put in jail for kidnapping. And other times—like today—she didn't bother. And sometimes—like today—she allowed Robin to stay as her brother and have a bedroom in the house too. But more times she sent him to jail with Granny Knott. That was the wonderful thing about daydreams; you could make them to order, like birthday cakes or pizzas, with fresh decorations and toppings to fit in with your mood.

The only drawback with daydreams was that they got interrupted. At school Jessica's teacher, Miss Forbes, was for ever interrupting. 'Anyone awake here?' she would joke first thing in the morning, knocking on the surface of Jessica's desk. By lunch time she had grown angry. 'Jessica,' she would slam her ruler down on the wood. 'I don't believe you've listened to a word I've said.'

At home the interruptions were even worse. Robin teased. Granny grumbled.

The oak tree was Jessica's answer to these problems. It was situated on her route home, at the corner of the Speedy Transport depot, where the right-hand wall of the car park met the road. Hidden high up, among its leaves and branches, she could daydream as much as she liked. And her hiding place had the added advantage of giving her a splendid view of the surrounding countryside. She could watch the bright orange Speedy lorries coming and going through the gates. More fascinating still, she could watch the comings and goings of the families who lived in the posh houses on the other side of the road.

Louise Witherspoon's house, Mount Arabis, was one of these.

Louise had been late home that afternoon. It was almost five o'clock when Jessica spotted Mrs Witherspoon's little red Metro nosing up the sweeping conifer-lined driveway. Eagerly she peered at the two figures alighting on the gravel; Louise, so golden and dainty, her mother so elegant and tall. They were carrying parcels. New clothes probably. Jessica watched them pass out of sight through the arched doorway and, as she watched, she felt her daydream go as cold as yesterday's cabbage.

There were six bedrooms, four bathrooms and a swimming-pool behind Mount Arabis' gleaming white-pillared façade. Jessica had an imaginary mansion, but Louise had the real thing.

She didn't see much point in staying in her special hiding place after that. And in any case, she was hungry. Slowly she swung to the ground. With a bit of luck, Granny Knott would have forgotten about the bruises on her cucumbers, and remembered to put some potatoes on to boil.

A wonderful mouth-watering smell hit her the moment she opened the caravan door. Robin was stretched out across the settee stuffing himself with chips.

'Ooo. Give us one. Did Gran get you those? Are there any for me?' She made a grab for the packet.

Her brother fended her off with one large bare foot. 'Go on out there an' ask her.' He waved a greasy hand in the direction of the vegetable garden.

'Granny! Granny! I want chips!' Yelling at the top of her voice, Jessica raced back down the steps towards the long plastic tunnel where Granny Knott grew her tomatoes.

It wasn't until she was half-way across the cabbage patch that she realised her mistake. Two figures were coming out of the tunnel in answer to her call. Granny wasn't alone. She had a visitor. Normally when strangers were around (and strangers meant everyone except Granny and Robin) Jessica wouldn't have spoken above a whisper.

'So this is Jessica.' The stranger held out her hand. 'Hello, dear. I'm Isabel Lovett.'

Jessica just looked up long enough to catch a glimpse of a very small person with a very bright smile, before dropping her eyes and shuffling backwards.

'Like I was tellin' you, she's no talker,' shrugged Granny Knott. 'And you'd get more action from a lame donkey. But if she can be any use til you, you're welcome.'

What was going on? In spite of herself, Jessica shot Mrs Lovett a quick, questioning glance.

'Have you ever heard of Brownies, dear?' the visitor asked.

Jessica dropped her eyes again and shook her head, even though this wasn't quite true. Louise and the three Rs had all started Brownies the week before. They had got told off for chattering about it in class.

'It's a sort of club for girls aged seven to ten,' Mrs Lovett explained. 'We meet in the church hall at half-past six on Friday evenings.'

'You'll be startin' a lot later if you're waiting for that one to turn in. She's never been one for socialising,' said Granny Knott.

'Do come, Jessica,' Mrs Lovett pleaded. 'Quite a few of your school friends will be there. You'd enjoy the fun.'

She made it sound so easy. As if Jessica could simply show up at the hall and join in. As if she had friends like everyone else.

'I brought something for you.' The visitor was now reaching into the depths of her carrier bag, fishing out a shiny blue book. 'It's a copy of the Brownie Handbook. Sharon got two of them as presents when the uniform changed, so you needn't give it back. We'll be looking at the Brownie Story in the Beginners' Group next week.'

She had hit on something Jessica could not

resist. The girl loved books with pictures. Library time was the one hour on the school timetable when Miss Forbes didn't have to knock on her desk for attention.

And suddenly, standing there, with a brand new book of her own between her hands, Jessica felt a surge of hope and excitement. Perhaps Brownies would be different. Perhaps at Brownies it wouldn't matter that she didn't live in a proper house with nice clothes and a mummy like Louise and Rachel and Rosie and Ruth. Perhaps, just perhaps, Brownies could make her daydreams come true.

'You will come, won't you, dear?' Mrs Lovett's smile was brighter than ever.

Jessica retreated three paces, still clutching her book. She couldn't bring herself to open her mouth.

But this time she nodded.

2

First Night

BY FRIDAY GRANNY KNOTT had forgotten all about the Guider's visit.

'I don't care if the archangel Gabriel came and invited ye til heaven. You're not goin' anywhere until you've bagged them carrots,' she declared when Jessica tried to slip out of the van after tea.

There was a whole sackful of carrots to be put into bags—all damp and earthy with the leaves still on—but somehow Jessica managed to finish the awkward messy job in record time. By half-past six she was racing up the pebbled side-path of St Peter's parish church.

Shyly she peeped round the door of the hall. She saw a long wooden-floored room with windows on one side, a platform at the top and what looked like hundreds of girls in brown and yellow uniforms all racing around.

'Jessica!' A familiar voice cried, and a small figure in blue came tripping towards her, just in time to stop her running away as fast as she'd come.

And from the other side of the room bounded a tall athletic-looking Brownie with straight brown hair and sticking-out teeth.

'Hi, you must be Jessica. I'm Sharon. Mum's put you in my Six.'

'That's right,' Mrs Lovett arrived, panting slightly, a little behind her daughter. 'You're going to be a Pixie.'

Jessica felt a bubble of happiness rise within her. She already knew from her handbook that Brownies were divided into groups called Sixes. And here she was within five seconds of her arrival with a Six and a Sixer all of her own. But before the warmth of this welcome could wipe the worried frown off her face, she caught sight of Louise and the three Rs in a huddle under the window. Unlike the rest of the Brownies, they weren't in uniform (although Louise wore a pale primrose track-suit with matching socks—clearly the next best thing). Rosie was mouthing: 'Oh no! It's Beansprout!' Rachel and Ruth were looking amazed. And Louise was pinching her pretty little nose between the finger and thumb of her right hand as if something smelled nasty.

Splat. The bubble of happiness burst. Jessica hung her head and shied away from Sharon's friendly tug on her sleeve.

It was true. She was dirty. She had come straight from Granny's vegetable patch, with mud on her shoes and a hole in her jeans. She hadn't even taken time to wash the carrot juice off her hands.

From that moment there was no question of Jessica even *trying* to join in. She knew what would happen. No one would want to stand next to someone with dirty orange-stained hands in the circle; no one would want a partner with dirty orange-stained hands for the games. Sharon might as well have pulled on the arm of a marble statue.

'What'll I do? She won't move,' the Sixer appealed to her mother.

Mrs Lovett placed her hands on Jessica's shoulder. 'Perhaps she'd rather watch for a while. There's no need to rush things.' Then gently, without any rushing, she steered Jessica to the back of the hall and lifted her up onto a table.

From that place of safety Jessica observed her first Brownie meeting: the Brownie Ring, prayers, games. It was all exactly as she'd read in her handbook. Little by little she began to relax.

'Time to get into your groups now, Brownies,' Mrs Lovett announced.

At this everyone started pulling chairs to various parts of the hall. Sharon and the other big girls climbed onto the platform. Another group gathered around the fire exit, while a third made a circle under the windows. Louise and the three Rs stood with Mrs Lovett beside the door.

Suddenly, to Jessica's dismay, the Guider waved over at her.

'Yoo-hoo, we're coming to join you,' she called, leading her Beginners' Group across the hall.

Oh no! Jessica hunched her back and folded her arms tight across her chest, like a snail drawing into its shell. She didn't look up. Not even when Louise and the three Rs put their chairs in a semi-circle round her table and Mrs Lovett placed a hand on her knee for a little welcoming speech.

'You know Jessica, don't you girls? I just want to say how glad we are to have her with us in Brownies.'

There was a brief silence in which Jessica felt sure her classmates were looking anything but glad.

'So, let's see what you remember from last week,' the Guider continued cheerfully.

'We learned that the way to become Brownies is by making the Brownie Promise,' Louise piped up.

'Well done, Louise. Now, Ruth, can you tell me three things a Brownie needs to do before making her Promise?'

Before Ruth could answer Louise piped up again: 'Hear or read the story of the Brownies. Know how to wear our uniform. And understand the Law and Promise. Please, Mrs Lovett, Mummy says I've done all those things. Can I make my Promise next week?'

'This isn't a race,' the Guider laughed. 'I like my Brownies to spend at least four weeks preparing for their Promise Ceremony.'

'Four weeks!' Louise made it sound like a life sentence.

'Cheer up,' smiled Mrs Lovett. 'There'll be plenty to keep you busy. You've your Promise Badge Book to fill in for a start.'

Another new book? Hopefully Jessica peered out under her eyebrows, still without raising her head. Yes. The Guider had taken a pile of yellow booklets from a brown paper bag.

Setting them to one side, she told the group what she wanted them to do for the following week.

'The Brownie story shows us that Brownies, above everything else, are meant to be helpful,' she explained. 'So for next week I want you to see how many times you can lend a hand. You'll find a page for drawing pictures of your Good Turns in your Brownie Promise Books.'

Immediately everyone started talking about the different helpful things they could do. As usual Louise was full of ideas; she could answer the telephone, turn on the microwave, stack the dish-washer, clear glasses from the tables beside the swimming-pool.

Jessica listened, in a daze of admiration. Louise was so pretty, with her soft golden curls, pink and white skin and huge blue eyes. No wonder Mr Witherspoon called her Princess and Miss Forbes had given her the leading part in their class play.

As a further sign of her star quality, Louise hit on a way of lending a hand there and then.

'I'll give the Promise Badge Books out for you, Mrs Lovett,' she piped.

'Thank you, dear. There should be one for everybody.'

Jessica's heart leapt at these words. But once again in a matter of moments she was made to remember how unBrownie-like she was. . . .

'One for me, one for Rachel, one for Rosie, one for Ruth,' Louise murmured as she passed the booklets round the circle. Then instead of handing the fifth one to Jessica, she gave it back to Mrs Lovett.

'No point in wasting this on Beansprout,' she said sweetly. 'She's too dreamy to help anyone. All she ever does is sit and stare into space.'

'Of course she must have one!' Mrs Lovett exclaimed. 'I happen to know that Jessica helps her grandmother in all sorts of ways.'

Louise was unimpressed. 'Well, she didn't help much last week. She ran off and left the poor old woman pushing a whole trolley-load of vegetables home on her own.'

'And did *you* offer to lend a hand in her place?' the Guider enquired quietly.

Taken aback for once, the star Brownie-to-be fiddled with the medallion on her spotless tracksuit. 'I would have, but I had to stay clean to

24

help with shopping,' she pouted. 'And you see, Jessica's granny is like Jessica—she doesn't wash.'

'Wasn't that a terrible thing to say!' The meeting was over and Mrs Lovett was following Sharon into the rectory kitchen, shedding bags of equipment as she went.

Sharon put on the kettle.

'Louise Witherspoon is a real pain. She's the one Brownie in the whole Pack I really can't stand. It would have been OK if Jessica had come with me to the Six corner. All the girls in my Six are really nice.'

Just at that moment Mr Lovett, the Rector, popped his head round the door. He was a thin balding man with a rather solemn face which lightened amazingly when he smiled.

'If you're asking do I want tea, the answer is "yes",' he said.

Mrs Lovett lifted a third mug from the mug rack and placed it on the table.

'You've arrived just in time for the moan-in,' sighed Sharon.

'Oh dear. Sounds gloomy. What went wrong?'

'Everything!' said Sharon, with a dramatic flourish of the teapot. 'Jessica—the girl we were telling you about—came to Brownies and probably hated every minute. She sat on her own in a corner and slipped out before the end.'

'Oh dear!' said her father again in a solemn tone.

Mrs Lovett gave a little flutter of impatience. '"Oh dear!" Is that all you can say? Something ought to be *done*. The child's grandmother isn't capable of looking after two children. Her mind's starting to wander . . .'

'Well you *are* doing something, aren't you?' Mr Lovett sipped his tea.

'Yes. But it won't be enough.'

'It never is.' Her husband consulted his diary. 'Ooops.' He unfolded his long awkward legs. 'I shouldn't be here. I have a prayer meeting.'

'I'm sure I could have stopped Jessica hating Brownies if it hadn't been for Louise Witherspoon,' muttered Sharon as he left the room.

The Lovetts would have been flabbergasted if they had known how Jessica really felt about the Brownie meeting. She certainly hadn't hated it. True, she hadn't been able to join in that first night because of her dirty hands. But she had come away with so much to think about—what the Guider had said in the Beginners' Group, what had been said in prayers. At long last, it seemed, she was on the right track, discovering what she needed to do to make friends.

The only obstacle to progress was Granny Knott.

'You needn't think you're going til flit off every Friday night in life on this Brownie lark,' the old lady had warned grumpily as she slipped through the door of the mobile home.

26

'God knows there's enough young ones parading around in fancy uniforms without you joining in.'

The threat had only served to make her granddaughter more determined.

There were eight turnips and a cauliflower on her bunk bed when she finally turned in for the night, but for once the stray vegetables didn't upset her. So what if Louise Witherspoon always climbed into a perfectly made bed with a frilly pink valance and matching duvet? Tonight Jessica believed she had found a way to bridge the gap between them. In the darkness she held her Brownie Promise Book between her hands and thought of the clean blank page waiting for her 'Lend a Hand' drawings. How would she fill it? What sort of helpful things could she do in the mobile home? Still chewing over the juicy question of her very first Good Turn, she fell asleep.

3

Mr Witherspoon

JESSICA CRAWLED OUT of her bunk-bed next
morning with a picture from the Brownie story
in her mind. It was of Tommy and Betty's
mother hugging her two helpful children. Tommy
and Betty had made such a change in *their*
house when Betty began to be a Brownie. They
had got up bright and early that first morning
and washed dishes and brushed the floor and
tidied up toys and put their clothes away.

I'll do exactly the same, Jessica thought, as
she made her way into the living area. I'll tidy
up the whole place so that if anyone comes to
visit they'll know a Brownie lives here.

But it wasn't that simple. Five minutes into
her first Good Turn, Jessica almost gave up.
She couldn't wash dishes because yesterday's
tea had been chips from the take-away. She
couldn't brush the floor because it was covered
in boxes of vegetables. She couldn't tidy up toys
because the only place to tidy them was into
cupboards crammed full of tinned foods. As for

folding up clothes—well, there weren't any piles of clean washing lying around—just Robin's grubby jeans and T-shirt. She'd have them folded in ten seconds flat. . . .

As she lifted the limp, faded denims, she glanced at the clock. Her expression changed. Nine o'clock! Those jeans shouldn't be on the floor at this hour of the morning, they should be down at Witherspoon's Service Station—on Robin.

For the last six months her brother had had a part-time job. Every Friday evening Mr Witherspoon would park his Porsche beside the service station car-wash. And first thing on Saturday morning Robin would hose the car down, then polish it with a chamois till it gleamed. He earned five pounds a week that way and had almost saved enough for a Raleigh Aztec mountain bike. But Granny Knott kept forgetting to wake him up.

'Robin! Robin!' Jessica hammered on the thin wooden partition which cut off her brother's box-size bedroom from the living-area. 'You've slept in again!'

From the other side of the partition came a groan, followed by Robin's sleep-flushed face.

'Oh no! I've blown it!' He stumbled into the living room and sprawled among the vegetables. 'Withers'll fire me this time for sure.'

Jessica looked at him with annoyance. In the Brownie story, Betty's brother Tommy had

29

been as quick as his sister to see what was wrong with their old untidy ways. But Robin certainly wasn't going to make it any easier for *her* to be a Brownie. Just because he was fourteen and big for his age, Robin thought he could do what he liked—which was next to nothing. He slouched around. He let Granny wait on him. He got dreadful school reports because he never bothered with homework. Up to now Jessica hadn't particularly minded. Turnips were turnips. Robin was Robin. You didn't expect them to be anything else. But this morning it was different. This morning the last thing she wanted was a useless layabout brother who got fired from his Saturday job.

'Quick! Put those on and go!' She flung him the jeans.

'It's hopeless, Jess,' Robin groaned. 'Old Withers will sack me before I even turn on the hose.'

'He might be late. You might get the car finished. You'll never know if you don't *try*.' She threw the T-shirt as she spoke.

He made a half-hearted attempt to catch it and missed. The shirt landed on the table and knocked over a milk bottle. It was two-thirds empty, but the remaining third began to trickle its way to the edge and drip down into one of the boxes on the floor.

'It's hopeless, I tell you. Withers is *never* late.'

Jessica looked at the trickling milk and felt

tears of frustration prick the back of her eyes. It wasn't hopeless. It couldn't be hopeless.

'I'll ... I'll *keep* him late,' she declared suddenly, and then gasped as if she could hardly believe what she'd said.

'Keep him late!' Her brother's face cracked into an incredulous smile. 'You!'

'How long do you need?'

'Half an hour.' Slowly Robin began to haul his jeans on over his pyjamas. He was looking at her with a new expression in his eyes. 'Do you really think you can pull it off?'

The honest answer was 'no'. Reg Witherspoon was a huge man. It would take the back end of a rugby team to keep him from jogging the five hundred yards from Mount Arabis to the car wash in his usual three minutes. But Jessica was so caught up in the desire to make things better (or at least to stop them getting worse) she didn't care. 'I can try,' she said firmly.

'Right.' Robin scrambled into the rest of his clothes.

'Right.' His sister armed herself with a large head of cabbage. (She had no clear plans for using it, but it made her feel brave.)

'Come on, then.'

'Shh. There's Gran.'

Scarcely daring to breathe they crept past the bent dungareed figure in the vegetable-patch. They were almost through the gate by the time she saw them, and by then it was too late for her to do anything except wave her trowel and yell.

'Where do yous think yous are going at this hour of the night? It's way past your bed-time. Get back into that van!'

'Wish me luck,' said Jessica.

'You've got it.' Her brother directed the jet of the power hose onto the brilliant red body of the car. 'Now scoot!'

With an unreal feeling, Jessica scooted out onto the footpath. She hadn't a clue what she would do if she saw Louise's father's big broad body striding towards her down the road. Run in the opposite direction probably, a shaky little voice whispered inside her head. Fortunately there was no sign of him. She turned right and managed to reach her oak tree unchallenged. But then, just as she was beginning to hope she could relax into a peaceful daydream for the next twenty-five minutes, the front door of Mount Arabis opened, and Reginald Witherspoon filled the porch.

He was even broader than Jessica remembered. With his bristling black beard, red tie and dazzling white shirt, he could have passed for Santa Claus' younger brother. But one look at the set of those bushy black eyebrows as he strode down the driveway, reminded her that Reginald Witherspoon—millionaire owner of Witherspoon's Service Station and of Speedy

Transport—was not the sort of man to greet would-be Brownies with a cheery 'ho ho ho'.

To her relief he didn't head straight for the service station. Instead he made his way in through the gates of the depot and strode towards the office.

Again she crossed her fingers, hoping that whatever business was taking Mr Witherspoon to the heart of his empire would keep him there for the next twenty minutes. Again she was disappointed.

'Deal with those letters for me, would you Pam?' His voice boomed through the open office window. 'I'm off to pick up the Porsche.'

That was it. She moved. Fast. Down the tree. Over the fence.

And suddenly she was at the door of the office. She was looking inside. Reginald Witherspoon was staring straight back at her, raising his ferocious eyebrows, waiting for her to speak.

'Well, what have we here?' he boomed.

Jessica did the only thing she could do under the circumstances. She held out her cabbage.

It seemed to shrink to the size of a seasick grapefruit between his big broad hands. 'Do you know anything about this piece of merchandise, Pam?' he demanded.

'Certainly not. It's nothing to do with me. I don't even *like* the stuff,' the bespectacled woman behind the desk replied hurriedly.

It was the spectacles and the desk that gave

the girl her inspiration, reminding her of school, of Miss Ford, and the class projects she'd talked about the previous week.

'P-please c-can you tell me about your lorries,' Jessica whispered. 'I'm doing a project in school.'

If a TV film crew had just rolled up at the door the change in Mr Witherspoon could not have been more remarkable.

He looked flattered. 'A school project, eh? Hear that, Pam?'

'Very nice.' Pam dutifully rearranged her face from irritated to pleased. 'So what do you need to know, dear?'

'Umm . . .' What Jessica needed was enough information to keep Robin's boss in the office for twenty minutes. She decided to play safe. 'Umm . . . everything.'

'Everything!' Mr Witherspoon slapped his knee. 'The girl wants to know everything. The Speedy Transport story from beginning to end. Well, let me tell you this, young lady. Speedy Transport begins and ends *here*!' He thumped his chest. 'You're talking to a self-made man. Reg Witherspoon started it. Reg Witherspoon owns it. Reg Witherspoon runs it. And Reg Witherspoon has made it into what it is today. The most efficient transport company in Ireland, studied in schools the length and breadth of the land.'

Jessica's eyes widened. She couldn't think what to say, so she said nothing, which was all the encouragement Reg Witherspoon needed to keep talking. He pulled up a packing case for her to sit on, lit a cigar and parked his bottom on the edge of Pam's desk.

It was a full forty minutes before she was back under her tree.

Like a red streak of lightning Withers' Porsche flashed past.

'Jessie! You're a wonder!' Robin was loping down the road towards her. 'I got the whole job done ... boot, bonnet, lights, windows, the lot. I was hanging about, twiddling my thumbs when yer man finally rolled in. Come on.' He grabbed her arm. 'This calls for a milk-shake.'

What a sweet, sweet taste! They sat together in the café, and for once, Jessica had something to say. In fact she bubbled over with information.

'Do you know what? Withers is a self-made man. But that doesn't mean he sewed the hairs on his chest. It means he started with no money.

'Do you know what? He works a ninety-eight hour week and owns eighty lorries and ten of his drivers are women.

'Do you know what? He's worried about vandals. There's some gang slashed a whole load of tyres last week.'

Robin hadn't known any of these things.

'You're a wonder, Jess,' he repeated in the end, running his big hands through his thick ginger mop in amazement. 'Who'd have guessed you had it in you?'

'You never know what you can do until you *try*.' Jessica lectured him firmly but shyly (since she'd only just discovered it herself).

They stood for a while outside the bicycle shop before going home.

The purple and yellow Raleigh Aztec was still in the window.

'Twenty-one speed gears,' Robin murmured reverently. 'Look at that frame! Those handlebars! Those fantastic graphics!'

'How much more money do you need?'

Her brother took out a biro and did some calculations on the palm of his hand. 'Eighteen pounds seventy-five pence,' he said in a voice full of longing. 'Four weeks and I could be sitting on that saddle. I dream of it at nights.'

'I've a dream that'll take four weeks too,' Jessica nodded.

She was thinking of Brownies. She felt like running straight round to Mrs Lovett's to tell her the good news. After a shaky start she had pulled off her first Good Turn. A bit different from Tommy and Betty's, of course. Not the sort of soap and water thing that Brownies were meant to start with. But still, a brilliant success. Her own brother had grabbed her arm and said she was 'a wonder'. And this was just the beginning. Now she knew it wasn't hopeless, she would go on to try all sorts of other things. . . .

And perhaps, just *perhaps*, by the time she made her Promise, Louise Witherspoon would think she was 'a wonder' too.

4

Invitations

WITH HER TONGUE poking slightly out of the corner of her mouth, Jessica put the finishing touches to the drawing. She coloured her own hair brown and Mr Witherspoon's tie red. Then she realised she didn't have a green felt-tip for the cabbage, so she licked the end of a dried-out black one, and coloured it a watery purple instead.

Just as she finished the bell rang and Louise and the three Rs burst into the classroom.

'Look! Beansprout's working on her Brownie Promise Book!' Rosie nudged Ruth.

The two girls giggled and pranced over to the table. Immediately Jessica covered the page with her hands.

'Go on. Let us see it.' With a deft flick of the wrist, Ruth caught an edge of the booklet and pulled the picture into view.

'Hey!' A note of surprise crept into her voice. 'That's good. You're good at drawing, Beansprout.'

Jessica blinked. Was there some kind of Brownie magic at work? Suddenly people were praising her! First Robin, now Ruth. She took a closer look at her drawing. Yes, she decided, it *was* good. The man looked like a man, and the girl looked like a girl, and the cabbage looked like a cabbage. Less convincing pieces of artwork had been pinned on the classroom wall.

'Jessica! You're not listening! What did I just say?'

Jessica sighed. It was after lunch—the time Miss Forbes got cranky.

'Umm ... umm ... you said ... umm. ...'

'I said get out your project notebooks. Now pay attention,' the teacher snapped. 'Hands up all those who have started their projects already.'

To her amazement Jessica found herself raising her hand.

'Goodness ... er ... Jessica, would you like to tell us what your project is about?' Miss Forbes seemed amazed too.

'Transport, Miss Forbes.'

'What an excellent idea!' If Jessica had announced she was planning a world tour, her teacher couldn't have shown more enthusiasm. 'Are we thinking of transport through the ages, dear?'

'No ... umm ... just through Ireland.'

'And have you got some library books to help you?'

39

'No ... umm ... I've talked to Mr Wither-spoon about his lorries.'

'Well, I must say I'm delighted to see you taking such an interest. Well done, Jessica. Keep it up.'

'Please ... Miss Forbes ... please ... please ...'

As Jessica sat, glowing with pleasure and surprise, Louise almost waved her arm off her shoulder in her eagerness to claim the teacher's attention.

'Please, Miss Forbes, I've got an excellent idea too.'

Louise's excellent idea turned out to be a project on invitations. Her mummy and daddy got invited out all the time, she explained—to lunches and dinners and openings and exhibitions. They'd even been invited to a garden party in Hillsborough Castle. And the Prince of Wales had been there. And now Louise was planning to stick all their different invitations in her project book and write about them, and say the sort of things it was important to put on invitations, like RSVP if you wanted a reply. And she was planning to include some invitations she had designed, ones which could be used for children's birthday parties. And she was going to pick the nicest design and use it for her own invitations to her birthday party the following week ... and it would have to be RSVP of course because her mummy would need to know how many ice-cream tubs to

order and how many going-home presents to
buy and . . .

'Well done, Louise,' Miss Forbes managed to
squeeze in a word. 'You've plenty to keep you
busy there. Now pencils and crayons out,
everyone, and thinking-caps on. I want to see
twenty-nine beautifully illustrated project titles
before you go home.'

For once Jessica settled down to work with
enthusiasm. She spent the next twenty minutes
printing Speedy Transport in large watery
purple capitals. Then she began to draw a line
of orange lorries zooming through the gap
between the words.

She might have got the depot drawn as well
if it hadn't been for the drama on the other side
of the table. Louise was breaking off her special
friendship with Ruth. There was nothing un-
usual about this. Although Louise and the three
Rs went around together, Louise always picked
one of the three to be her special friend. For a
few weeks the pair would be inseparable, chattering and giggling and sitting together all the
time. And then, without warning, Louise would
dump Rosie in favour of Rachel, or dump
Rachel in favour of Ruth. Today it was Ruth's
turned to be dumped. When Ruth made a joke,
Louise didn't laugh; when she asked a question,
Louise didn't answer; and when she showed
Louise the title of her project, Louise turned up
her nose.

'Not another project on cats,' she sighed. 'Cats are so *common*.'

'Invitations are commoner and a lot less use,' Ruth hissed back. 'You said so yourself. Your parents get hundreds of invitations every year, but they've only got one cat. And if a mouse got into your bedroom, you wouldn't send an invitation up to catch it!'

'We don't *have* mice in *our* house,' Louise sniffed.

At this point Miss Forbes tapped her pencil on her desk and glared.

'Please, Miss Forbes, Ruth's keeping me back,' cried Louise.

'Please, Miss Forbes, there's an empty place beside Jessica. Can I move?' cried Ruth.

'Girls, girls!' The teacher rolled her eyes. 'Very well, Ruth, move if you wish—but do it *quietly*.'

It was a long time since Jessica had had anyone sitting beside her.

'I bet you hate Louise,' Ruth whispered as she slipped into the empty chair. 'I do.'

Hate Louise? Jessica fiddled with her pencil. The word made her feel uncomfortable. She would never have dared to say: 'I hate Louise.' The only person Louise made her hate was herself.

Fortunately Ruth had switched her attention to other matters.

'I hate drawing too,' she moaned. 'Your

lorries look so real you'd expect them to drive off the page. But my stupid cat looks like a clothes-peg. Its front legs are growing out of its chin.'

'I'll fix them for you,' Jessica offered.

'Thanks a million. Do you want the lend of my black felt-tip for your wheels?'

They worked on in a companionable silence during which Jessica transformed Ruth's cat, finished her own title page and started work on a new picture in her Brownie Promise Book.

She had never known an afternoon pass so happily and so quickly. 'It can't be that time!' she gasped when Miss Forbes told the class to pack up.

Brrring! The bell rang shrilly.

Wham! Like a ball on the rebound, Louise dashed round to Ruth's side of the desk.

'So you'd rather sit beside Jessica than me, and you think my invitations are common,' she spat. 'OK then. Let's see how you like this. I'm inviting Jessica to my party instead of you!'

'I'm inviting Jessica to my party.' 'I'm inviting Jessica to my party.' The words repeated themselves over and over again in Jessica's head—words full of Brownie magic, the sweetest, most beautiful words she had ever heard in her life. Every day after school, she sat in her tree and savoured their meaning.

She was going to a party. The most wonderful

party in the whole world, with a swimming pool and ice-cream and going-home presents and sausages and. . . .

Every day at news-time Louise added further wonders to the list. On Tuesday she had gone to Belfast with her mummy to order a specially designed cake. On Wednesday they'd booked a conjurer (who'd been on TV). On Thursday they'd bought proper little trophies as prizes for the surprise competition.

And then it was Friday. And Louise was tantalisingly busy and mysterious. She didn't say a word at news-time. She just sat at the back of the classroom with a pile of little cards half-hidden on her knee. Every now and then, she'd slip one onto the table and disappear behind the encircling shield of her arm to write.

'Shh. Don't interrupt. I'm trying to finish these invitations in time to give them out tonight at Brownies,' Jessica overheard her whisper in Rosie's ear.

It would have taken an earthquake to keep Jessica away from the Brownie meeting after that.

Granny Knott wasn't an earthquake. But she gave a fair impression of a rumbling volcano when she saw her granddaughter getting ready to go out.

'There's no call for all this washin' and brushin' and fussin' around. Sit down there, would ye, and take your tea,' she rumbled ominously.

'I explained, Granny. I'm going to Brownies,' Jessica gave one last scrub at her face and reached for her coat, terrified that if she waited a moment longer her grandmother would come up with some filthy job.

'You'll do as I say, girl. I told you last week, I don't hold with childer bandin' together in a group to walk the streets.'

'Brownies don't walk the streets,' cried Jessica. 'We stay in the church hall and play games. Please, Granny, I've got to go now or I'll be late.'

To her horror her grandmother stood up and bolted the door.

'Brownies are OK,' Robin spoke up unexpectedly on her behalf. 'You let Jessie go.'

'And just who do you think you are, Mr Know-all, tellin' your elders and betters what to do?' the old lady retorted. But she drew back the bolt. She was much more likely to do things when Robin asked.

Ten minutes later, relieved, breathless and with a pair of spotlessly clean hands, Jessica reached the church hall.

Louise had walked in just moments ahead of her. And yes—she'd brought a pile of pale pink envelopes.

'Please, Mrs Lovett. These are my birthday invitations. And Mummy said would it be all right if I gave them out at Brownies, because there are some Brownies I want to invite who aren't in my class at school?' she announced.

Mrs Lovett hesitated. For a moment it seemed she might turn down Mummy's request.

'I think the best plan would be for me to look after them for you until the meeting is over,' she said carefully. 'Then you can give them out when everyone's putting on their coats to go home.'

'Oh! All right,' Louise shrugged, clearly put out by this delay. 'I just hope I don't forget them. Mummy would be ever so cross.'

At least twenty times in the course of the next hour and a half Jessica glanced over at the little pile of pink envelopes sitting on the Guider's table. There was absolutely no danger of *her* forgetting they were there.

They seemed to be on Mrs Lovett's mind too. When the time came for prayers she read a bit from the Bible about a man who organised a huge party and invited a huge number of guests. But when the day came none of the people he'd invited turned up. So he sent his servants out into the streets and alleyways and invited all the beggars and down-and-outs to come to his party instead.

I bet Mrs Lovett picked that story to cheer up the Brownies who don't get an invitation from Louise, Jessica thought afterwards. She felt glad she wouldn't be one of them. Of course it was nice to know that God was keen on parties and invited the people who didn't get invited any-where else. But what good was a party in heaven in about a million years' time when you could have ice-cream and birthday cake and a conjurer in Mount Arabis next week?

She threw herself into the rest of the meeting, determined to show Louise how much becoming a Brownie had changed her. She didn't allow herself to daydream, not for a single minute. Steadily, if shyly, she listened, she laughed, she chatted with her Six. The highlight of her evening came in the Beginners' Group when Mrs Lovett saw her Promise Badge Book.

'Well done, Jessica.' The Guider looked as if she'd swallowed a light bulb, her smile was so bright. 'I'm *delighted* with your progress.'

There was just one awkward moment. Jessica couldn't risk telling the true story of her first 'Lend a Hand' drawing in front of Louise, so she said it was a picture of her talking to a man.

'Oh but you mustn't talk to strangers, dear. It isn't safe,' Mrs Lovett cried. 'Promise me you won't ever do that again.'

Shamefaced, Jessica promised and the discussion turned to Brownie uniforms. By this stage it was almost eight o'clock.

'My goodness!' Mrs Lovett suddenly glanced at her watch. 'The evening's flown! Quickly, girls—back into the circle. It's time for Brownie Bells.'

A few minutes later the words of the closing song filled the hall.

'O Lord our God, your children call,
Grant us your peace and bless us all.'

Jessica didn't join in. A huge lump of nervous excitement seemed to have moved up from her tummy to her throat. Louise was standing on the opposite side of the circle in front of the table. All she had to do was make a ninety-degree turn to pick up the invitations.

'Good night, Brownies,' said Mrs Lovett.

'Good night, Mrs Lovett,' the Brownies chorused.

At last—this was it! Everyone was running to get their coats. Louise was over at the Guider's table. She was holding the invitations. As Jessica watched, she checked the name on the top one, caught Ruth's arm and gave it to her.

Suddenly, Jessica felt a hand on her own shoulder. With a start, she turned round, and found herself looking up into Mrs Lovett's face.

'Come with me into the store, dear. We need to have a little chat,' the Guider smiled.

Oh no! Not now! Jessica jerked away. She would be out of sight in the store. Louise wouldn't know where to find her. But there was no getting out of it. Mrs Lovett had both hands on her shoulders and was half-pushing, half-steering her towards the door.

The chat was about uniforms.

48

'I just wanted you to know you needn't buy anything,' Mrs Lovett explained. 'Sharon's been growing so fast, we've still got all her old tops and bottoms at home.'

'Thank you very much, Mrs Lovett,' Jessica gasped. 'Please can I go now?'

'Not just yet.' The Guider produced a tape-measure. 'I want to check your measurements first.'

The measuring took for ever. Mrs Lovett wound the measure round Jessica's waist and bottom, then looked for a scrap of paper to write down the figures, then forgot what they were and had to take them all over again. When Jessica finally tore back into the hall, it was empty—apart from Sharon.

Jessica could have sat down on the floor and wept. Louise had gone home. She would have to wait until Monday now to get her invitation.

Why couldn't Mrs Lovett have picked some other time to fuss about stupid uniforms?

Mrs Lovett, of course, had known exactly what she was doing.

'You managed that brilliantly, Mum,' Sharon beamed as her mother locked the hall door.

The Guider pocketed her keys. 'I certainly wasn't going to stand around and give that spoilt little monkey another chance to leave Jessica out.'

'Yeah, it could have undone all the good work,' Sharon agreed. 'I mean Jessie really

seemed to enjoy herself tonight. She's come
right out of her shell.'

'She certainly got on well in the Beginners'
Group,' Mrs Lovett nodded.

'Mind you,' she frowned, 'I'm still worried.
I'm sure her grandmother doesn't know where
she is half the time. She could be doing
anything . . . talking to anyone. It isn't safe. . . .'

'Dear me!' A voice rang out behind them.
'Last week you were worried because Jessica
wasn't talking. And this week she's talking too
much. Some people are never satisfied.'

It was the third member of the Lovett family
on his way home from the church.

'Don't tease, Ralph,' said Mrs Lovett sternly.
'You know what I mean.'

'All I know is that I found this lying on the
pavement.' Ralph Lovett dipped his hand into
his pocket. 'Sharon really ought to be more
careful with her love letters.'

'A love letter! Sharon! You never told me!'

'Calm down, Mum. Dad's teasing again,' the
girl soothed. 'It's only my invitation to the spoilt
monkey's stupid party.'

5

At the Party

JESSICA WOKE UP next morning to the sound of a fierce argument going on outside her bedroom window. Robin and Granny Knott were bawling their heads off. For a moment she lay very still in her bunk bed, thinking what ugly voices they had, hoping the sound wouldn't carry. Then she sat up and pulled back the curtains.

Her grandmother was standing in the middle of the cabbage patch with her arms folded, while Robin stamped his feet and flailed his long arms, almost beside himself with rage.

'You owe me ten pounds,' he stamped. 'And I want it.' Stamp. *Now.*'

Granny Knott tossed her head. 'What you want is a good clip round the ear. Comin' home and demandin' the sun, moon and stars. Ten pounds indeed! I don't owe you the salt on a sausage!'

'You forgot to give me Mr Witherspoon's note.'

'Oh so I'm supposed to pay a small fortune for every wee thing as slips my mind now, am I? Let me tell you this, my lad. When you've got seventy-five years' worth of memories banging about in your brain, you'll forget the odd note too!'

Jessica poked her head out of the window.

'What's happened? It's after nine o'clock. Why isn't Robin at Witherspoon's?'

'Mind your own business, Miss,' Granny Knott retorted moving stiffly in the direction of her cabbages.

'I'll take the money out of your stocking,' Robin yelled after her.

When she didn't reply, he slumped down on the caravan steps.

'Old bag!' he muttered up at Jessica. 'Withers sent me a note to say he had to be away on business this weekend, and he'd pay double if I'd do the Porsche on Friday before he left. Only *she* forgot to give it to me until now. So I've lost my chance of a tenner, and I'm no closer to getting my bike.'

'It makes you want to kick someone.' Jessica could see he was feeling exactly the way she had felt the previous night after Mrs Lovett's measurements.

'Old people are so selfish,' she sighed.

She spent the rest of the weekend up her oak tree, counting the hours until Monday morning. The weather had lost its balmy late-summer warmth and there was an autumn chill in the air. Sometimes she surfaced from a daydream to find that her hands had turned blue and her feet had gone numb. But she stayed out of doors as long as possible—only returning to the mobile home at mealtimes, and when it got dark.

Over and over again she imagined herself walking up the sweeping driveway to knock on the front door of Mount Arabis. 'Excuse me,' she would greet Mrs Witherspoon politely. 'I've called for my invitation. I'm Jessica Knott.'

'Jessica. Of course! Come in, dear.' Mrs Witherspoon's frosty face would break into a welcoming smile. She would lift a silver tray from the mahogany hall table, on which would lie a single pink envelope. 'You are the one schoolfriend Louise really wants to see here on Thursday. You will come, won't you? Don't let us down.'

Meanwhile, in the real world, Robin remained in a temper and Granny Knott became more and more confused.

Jessica arrived home on Sunday evening to find her pouring cornflakes into bowls.

'Go to the shop an' get us a carton of milk, girl,' she ordered. 'Waiting on the milkman to deliver these mornings is like expecting a dead hen til lay eggs.'

'That's because it's seven o'clock in the evening. . . .' Jessica began—then stopped.

Her throat felt prickly and she was suddenly

too tired to explain. It was almost a relief to see the cereal bowls, for if her grandmother had been about to dish up a proper Sunday tea, she knew she couldn't have eaten a bite.

'I don't want anything. I'm not hungry,' she muttered. 'I'm going to bed.'

'Bed! *Bed!* Folks is going to bed in Australia, girl. They're getting up here.'

Ignoring her grandmother's ramblings, Jessica made her way to her bedroom where she crawled into her sleeping bag without bothering to undress. 'I can't be sick,' she told herself. 'I can't. I just can't.'

But she got up next morning feeling as if she had swallowed a load of sandpaper and the caravan had turned into a merry-go-round overnight. She had to hold on to the side of the bunk to steady herself as she struggled into her uniform. 'I can't be sick,' she kept telling herself. 'I've got to go to school to see Louise.'

Sheer determination carried her into the living-room and kept her upright long enough to swallow a few mouthfuls of tinned macaroni under Granny Knott's eagle eye. (At least it slipped down more easily than cornflakes.)

'I'm off now, Granny,' she croaked.

She made it as far as the door, and then the merry-go-round gathered speed. It was swirling her round, faster and faster. She felt her knees buckle and the macaroni rise in her throat.

'Jessie!' she heard Robin shout. And everything went black.

The next time she opened her eyes, she was lying across the long window seat at the front of the van, and Granny and Robin were arguing over her head. It took the girl a moment to realise that the argument this time was about her. Robin wanted to send for the doctor.

'Get away with you. There's not a thing wrong with her that a herb brew won't set right,' Granny Knott insisted.

Eugh! Jessica pulled a face. Granny's herb brews were supposed to cure everything from appendicitis to toothache. But they tasted like poison.

'I'm better. I'm going to school.' She tried to sit up.

'You're not!' Robin pushed her back down again.

'You'll stay where you are, girl!' Granny Knott agreed.

Jessica lay back on her pillow, feeling as if the whole world was against her.

'It isn't fair. I'm not sick. Just dizzy,' she croaked.

The dizziness continued over the next forty-eight hours. Days and nights jumbled together into a blur punctuated by revolting hot drinks from Granny Knott and Robin plonking himself down on her feet to ask if she was OK. She

lay for long periods in a fuzzy half-awake state
in which ordinary noises seemed a hundred
times louder than usual.

And then, at long last, her head cleared and
she understood that it was Wednesday morning
—the day before the party—and she had only
twenty-four hours left to get her invitation.

Robin found her crying into her pillow.

'I want to go to school, and I can't,' she
sobbed. 'My legs are too wobbly.'

'What do you expect?' Granny Knott waved
the frying-pan under her nose. 'You haven't
eaten for two days, girl. You're as green and
limp as a spring onion.'

Robin elbowed his grandmother out of the
way and put his mouth close to Jessica's ear so
that she was nearly knocked out with the smell
of the cheese and onion potato crisps he'd been
eating. 'Cheer up,' he whispered gruffly. 'I've a
surprise lined up for you this afternoon.'

His sister's sobs became sniffs. Secretly she
doubted whether his surprise was really worth
cheering up for, especially if it was a present
(Robin only ever gave things he wanted himself—
like screwdrivers and bicycle repair kits) but at
least, for once, he was trying.

She dozed on and off all day—her dreams
full of Louise and parties and pale pink envelopes. Shortly before four o'clock Granny Knott
bustled into her bedroom.

'Stir yourself, girl.' She dumped a box of

onions on the bottom of the bunk. 'You've got a visitor. There's a young one in the living-room has brought something for you.'

Jessica's heart leapt and she almost ran through the door. Dainty golden Louise come in person to deliver her invitation. It seemed too good to be true.

It was. The visitor turned out to be Sharon.

'Hi, Jessie.' She smiled her broad toothy smile and held out a large plastic bag. 'Robin told me you were sick, so I brought a few bits and pieces to help pass the time.'

'Thanks.' Disappointment sapped the strength from Jessica's legs. She sat down, not trusting herself to move another step. Her eyes widened as she saw the array of goods coming out of Sharon's bag: Brownie magazines, felt-tips, a children's Bible, two sets of Brownie T-shirts and sweat-pants, and a large box of chocolates.

'Mum sent those,' the Sixer explained. 'She won them at a Beetle Drive. But she doesn't want me to get spots, or herself to get fat, or Dad to get a heart-attack, so she's passing them on. You're not likely to get any of those things,' she finished kindly.

Jessica managed a smile ... which suddenly broadened as the luxurious assortment triggered an idea in her head. A bold plan of action. But could she? Dare she?

She ran over to Sharon. 'Quick. Give them to me.' She almost snatched the box out of her hands, then dived back into her bedroom. It was her last chance after all, and for her plan to stand any hope of success, she had to keep those chocolates hidden from Robin. . . .

Completely unsuspecting, Robin looked into her bedroom next morning to find her propped up in bed, surrounded by Brownie magazines.

'Raise the flag!' he cheered. 'My surprise worked. You look back to your normal awful self.'

'I'm not normal enough to go to school,' Jessica replied quickly. 'My legs still wobble.'

'Jellies wobble. But that never stopped them running,' Granny Knott muttered, not unkindly, from the sink.

'Any messages for Sharon?' Robin called before leaving.

'Tell her thanks for the stuff and I'll see her this . . . um . . . at Brownies.'

She had almost given herself away. But fortunately both Robin and Granny Knott were too pleased with her recovery to ask awkward questions. Her brother went on to school. Her grandmother went to market. And Jessica was left with a whole morning free to get on with her plan.

First she took the box of chocolates from its hiding-place under her pillow and wrapped it up in a brown paper bag decorated with a pattern of felt-tip daisies.

Then she washed her hair and changed into her best skirt—the one Granny had bought her from the Oxfam shop before she fell out with the volunteers. Fortunately it still fitted. Even more fortunately its blue and yellow swirls were a perfect match for the Brownie T-shirt Sharon had brought the day before.

Finally, while her hair was drying, she put the finishing touches to her card. The drawing on the front was of a group of Brownies in their Brownie ring. Now she added in two arrows—one pointing to a fair-haired Brownie and the other to the dark-haired Brownie by her side. At the top of the first arrow she wrote: 'YOU' and at the top of the second: 'ME'. 'To Louise. Happy Birthday. From your very good friend, Jessica,' she wrote inside.

Balloons hung like bunches of multi-coloured grapes around the front porch of Mount Arabis. From her hiding-place behind a rhododendron bush, Jessica watched them bob and sway as the front door opened and shut. She waited until the last of the parents' cars had driven away. Then, with the box of chocolates clasped to her chest, she made her own way to the door.

'What's this?' A stout woman in a floral overall responded to her knock.

Jessica stood on the doorstep, washed over by waves of enchantment. She heard music, laughter, clapping. Fairy lights twinkled round the ceiling. Furniture polish and sausages scented the air. Her pale cheeks flushed pink with excitement and her eyes shone.

'I'm here for the party,' she said in a small clear voice. 'I'm Jessica Knott.'

'Oh! Is Mrs Witherspoon a friend of your mummy's then?'

'I haven't got a mummy,' said Jessica. 'But my granny said I could come.'

Still the woman didn't say the magic words.

'What's wrong, Mary?' At that moment Mrs Witherspoon herself floated out of the kitchen carrying a plate of eclairs.

'There be's a child here looking to come to the party, but ... well ... you can see for yourself. . . .'

Louise's mother came to the door and looked.

She smiled. But it wasn't the warm welcoming smile that set everything right. It was the distant smile of a stranger. 'How can I help you?' she enquired.

Somehow Jessica managed to make her tongue work. 'Please. I've brought a present for Louise.' She held out the brown paper bag.

'How kind!' Mrs Witherspoon received it onto the tips of her beautifully manicured fingers.

'Mummy ... Mummy ...' A pair of double doors burst open and Louise skipped into the hall. Jessica's mouth dropped. From where she was standing she could now see into the heart

60

of the house, into the brilliantly-lit room where she so longed to be. But it wasn't at all as she had imagined. It looked like a pantomime stage. Her schoolmates were dressed up in masks ... clown costumes ... animal suits ... Louise herself wore a frothy ballet tutu and brandished a wand.

She pulled up short when she saw Jessica.

'What does *she* want?' she demanded in a very unballerina-like voice.

'Jessica called to wish you a happy birthday,' said Mrs Witherspoon. 'We could ask her to stay for the party but. ...'

'She'd look stupid,' finished Louise. 'It's fancy dress.'

'I'm s-sorry.' Jessica edged behind a pillar, desperate to remove her stupid skirt and T-shirt from view. 'I sh-shouldn't have come.'

'What? Are you going then, dear? Don't you want any cake? No ... well, goodbye then.'

Louise's mummy smiled a smile of frosty relief and shut the door.

6

A Brilliant Surprise

SHARON SLIPPED OVER to her mother's side. 'Have you seen Jessica?' she whispered.

'She was over there a moment ago.' Mrs Lovett glanced over to the corner of the hall where she had last noticed Jessica sitting staring into space, looking even paler than usual.

There was no sign of her now.

'We'd better check the cloakroom,' the Guider frowned. 'I thought the poor child seemed rather down in the dumps this evening, but I didn't get a chance to ask why.'

'I bet I know what's wrong with her,' said Sharon. 'She still feels bad about Louise's rotten party—about the way Mrs Witherspoon slammed the door in her face. I saw the whole thing from the lounge. It nearly made me sick.'

Even as she spoke, Louise came tripping towards them. She wore a badge with the words 'I am eight' pinned to her primrose track-suit. She was carrying a blue velvet jewellery case.

'Please, Mrs Lovett,' she smiled sweetly. 'I

brought the bracelet Daddy gave me yesterday for my birthday to show you. And please will you look after it for me until the end of the meeting, because it's nine carat gold and I'm helping make calendars for the church sale tomorrow and I don't want to get glue on the box?'

'Very nice.' The Guider barely glanced at the gleaming bracelet in its white satin nest, then snapped the case shut. 'Did you see where Jessica went?'

'Jessica? Oh, you mean *Beansprout*,' Louise giggled. 'I heard her saying she wasn't feeling well. She must have gone home.'

'Home?' Sharon and her mother exchanged glances.

'Go and take a look in the cloakroom, Sharon,' said Mrs Lovett. 'I'll ask one of the assistant Guiders to check outside.'

Jessica hadn't gone home. She had just slipped across the corridor into the main church building and was sitting there, in the back pew, looking round. She had never been inside St Peter's Church before. At one time Granny Knott had come regularly each Sunday. But the old church had been accidentally gutted by fire, and Granny Knott had stopped attending after that. 'You won't catch me in that new-fangled building,' she'd told the rector. 'With all that light wood and the ceiling so low, it puts me in mind of a coffin.'

As far as Jessica was concerned it was some-where to be miserable in peace. Watching Louise flit about the hall with her bracelet and hearing all her post-party chatter had made her feel like a worm. What was the point in trying to make her Brownie Promise? No matter how many Good Turns she did or how well she coloured in her Promise Badge Book, or how hard Sharon and Mrs Lovett tried to help her, she would never be accepted.

Everything about her was wrong. Her hair, her thinness, her clothes, her house, her family.

She sat huddled up in the corner of a pew rubbing her fists into her eyes. Any minute now Mrs Lovett and Sharon would come trying to cheer her up. She didn't want them to see her. In fact she didn't want *anyone* to see her—ever. She lowered her fists and looked round for somewhere to hide.

It was then she noticed the pattern on the floor. A beautiful, glowing pattern of light. She looked up and saw it was being caused by the last rays of the evening sun streaming through the stained-glass window on her left. The picture on the window was of a man on a cross.

She sat still, her attention captured. That's Jesus, she thought, remembering some of the things Mrs Lovett had said in prayers. Jesus was God's Son. He had come to earth and helped people and died on a cross and come back to life again, according to Mrs Lovett. And because he was alive he was someone who still helped people today.

The previous week Jessica had believed she had found a way of helping herself. But this week she was back to square one. For a long moment she considered the man in the window, with his outstretched arms and thorny crown. Was he really as obliging as Mrs Lovett made out? Would he be willing to help her? There were so many changes she wanted to be made in her life, she hardly knew where to begin.

'Please,' she moved three steps to the left, so the light was streaming down on to her face. 'Mrs Lovett says you know everything about everyone. But I don't expect you've noticed me. My name's Jessica and I'm really sorry for bothering you, but I could do with some help. I want to be like everyone else. I want my granny to stop forgetting things. And I want my brother to smarten up. And I want not to be teased and called names because of them. I want to get invited to parties and have friends like everyone else. . . .'

Before she could mention the name of the one special friend she had particularly in mind, she heard her Sixer call outside the door. 'Jessica! Jessica! You look in the cloakroom, Mum and I'll check the church.'

It was too late to hide. She kept her eyes fixed on the stained-glass window, determined not to move.

'I'd rather stay here,' she insisted when Mrs Lovett tried to persuade her to go back into the hall.

'OK then. I'll stay with you,' said Sharon.

Jessica sighed. Of course she liked Sharon. And she was grateful to her. But Sharon was too old to be a proper friend.

'Please, Mrs Lovett, my head hurts. Can I stay here too?' a voice piped.

Louise?! Scarcely able to believe her ears, Jessica stared at the small vibrant figure in the doorway.

'She's just trying to get out of making calendars, Mum,' hissed Sharon. 'Send her back to the hall.'

No ... no ... Jessica dug her nails into the palms of her hands.

And this time Mrs Lovett seemed to get the message. 'Come in, Louise,' she said cheerfully. 'Someone ought to keep Jessica company. So it might as well be you.'

'But *I'm* her Sixer,' Sharon protested.

'I know, dear. And the rest of your Six will be wondering where you are.' The Guider gripped her daughter by the arm and marched her across the pale blue carpet out through the door.

'Thank goodness for that,' said Louise. 'I've been trying to get you on your own all evening.'

'You have?' Now Jessica was sure that Jesus

66

had worked a miracle. As far as she could remember Louise had never even looked in her direction.

'Yes. I wanted to thank you for your card. I got fifty-seven cards, you know, and two book tokens—but yours was the only one that seemed really sincere.' Here Louise stopped and looked pathetic. 'I knew when you said you were my friend you really meant it.' She sighed. 'Rachel and Rosie and Ruth didn't mean the nice things they said on *their* cards. They're all so two-faced—not like you.'

'Two-faced?' Jessica felt a shy glimmer of curiosity mingled with pride.

'Yes. One minute they're friendly and the next . . . well . . . Do you know what Ruth said to me a moment ago in the hall?' Louise's voice rose in indignation. 'She said I was a show-off. And Rosie and Rachel agreed.'

'They're probably jealous,' said Jessica.

'Jealous? Of *me*?' Louise clasped her hands. 'Do you really think so?'

'It makes sense.' Jessica warmed to her theme. 'You're pretty and clever and you live in a big house and have lovely clothes and a swimming-pool and . . .'

'My daddy drives a Porsche. Yes . . . I see what you're getting at.' Louise nodded gravely. 'They don't have much in comparison. I mean, I heard Ruth's daddy's car failed the MOT and now he stays at home and her mummy goes to work by bus.'

She paused. Her voice rose. She placed a dainty hand on Jessica's arm. 'But that doesn't give her any excuse for being so nasty. I mean so what if my daddy's the richest man in Laganvale? It isn't my fault.'

'No, of course not,' Jessica gave her hand a squeeze.

'You're so understanding. I wish there were more girls like you,' sighed Louise.

Jessica pinched herself to make sure she wasn't dreaming. No. Her incredibly brilliant surprise was getting better and better. Louise invited her to hide from Rosie and Rachel and Ruth behind the pews.

So they crouched down, side by side, with their bottoms on kneelers and chatted as if they'd been best friends for years.

They talked about the Promise Ceremony. Louise felt that girls as two-faced as Rosie and Rachel and Ruth shouldn't be allowed to take part.

'It's still two weeks away. They might get more Brownie-like before then,' Jessica suggested.

Louise thought this unlikely. 'Still,' she settled into a more comfortable position on her kneeler, 'we can't go worrying about them. We have ourselves to think of.'

Louise was very good at thinking about herself. She had already thought through her preparations for the Promise Ceremony in great detail: what she would have for tea beforehand, how she would fix her hair, what time she would get into her uniform . . .

'And of course,' she finished, 'for such an important occasion I'll be wearing culottes.'

Jessica tried not to look shocked. She knew that Brownies had a choice of uniform. They could wear culottes instead of sweat pants, and polo shirts instead of T-shirts. But she had thought it all boiled down to the same thing.

Not according to Louise. For Promise Ceremonies, in Louise's opinion, culottes were the only suitable dress. Her mummy was going to give Mrs Lovett the money for hers after this week's meeting, and on Monday the Guider would be going to Guide Headquarters in Belfast to get them.

'I expect she'd get some for you too if you asked her,' Louise smiled a deliciously companionable smile. 'Rosie and Rachel and Ruth will probably wear sweat pants. It would be nice if at least two of us could be properly dressed.'

'Oh yes. Yes, it would,' Jessica breathed.

All too soon she heard the sound of feet and voices in the corridor. The Brownie Meeting was over.

'Louise! Jessica! Where are you?' Mrs Lovett called from the door.

'Over here.' The two girls popped up like Jack-in-the-boxes from the pew.

'Your mother is waiting at the door, Louise,'

Mrs Lovett smiled. 'And Jessica, your brother is in the hall.'

Robin! In the hall? Whatever did he want? Suddenly Jessica felt panicky. She didn't want Louise to see her with Robin. Quickly she changed the subject.

'Please will you get me Brownie culottes in Belfast?' she asked her Guider.

Mrs Lovett looked surprised. 'But you already have your uniform.'

'I know, but it's really Sharon's, and I want something of my own.'

'Well . . . in that case . . . I don't see why not. As long as your Granny is agreeable. Just drop the money in with me tomorrow.'

Tomorrow. That gave her twenty-four hours. Jessica sat on in the church for a few moments while the others stood chatting in the hallway—delighted, amazed, concerned. Her prayer had been heard. Help had been given. But was it enough? Louise was so changeable. She loved people one minute and hated them the next. It seemed to take so little to tip the balance.

For the second time that evening Jessica looked up at the stained-glass window.

'Please,' she prayed silently, 'don't let anything go wrong. Please let Granny Knott give me the money for culottes. And don't let Louise see me with Robin.'

Fortunately there was no sign of her brother

in the hall when she went out, just Sharon dangling her legs over the edge of the platform. 'If it's your brother you're looking for, he ran off when he saw me,' the Sixer called.

She found him outside the church gates, slouched against the railings. One look at his face was enough to take the edge off her pleasure and fuel her anxiety. He was in one of his sullen, teasing moods.

'About time too,' he greeted her with a scowl. 'Gran made me come and get you in case you collapsed on the road.'

'That's silly. I'm fine now. Come on. Let's go.'

'What's the hurry? You haven't even asked how I am.'

'So how are you?' Jessica tugged at his leather-jacketed arm. 'You can tell me on the way.'

Still her brother refused to budge. 'Ready to do Withers in, actually,' he scowled.

She cast a nervous glance over her shoulder. 'What's gone wrong?'

Robin shrugged. 'I've lost my job, that's what. He sacked me.'

'Oh no, Robin! *Why*?' She was truly appalled. All her efforts—and he ended up in trouble after all . . .

'He wanted the Porsche done last Friday and I didn't turn up.'

'But that was Granny's fault! She didn't give you the message.'

71

'Try telling him that. On second thoughts, don't bother. The truth is he was looking for an excuse to get rid of me.'

There was a silence while Jessica digested the news.

'What about the bike, then?' she said in a small voice.

'Work that out for yourself, genius.'

'You won't be getting it.'

'Did I say that?' said Robin. 'It's getting my own back on Withers that's the problem. I'll pick the bike up tomorrow.'

'But how will you pay?'

Her brother tapped the side of his nose.

'You're going to ask Granny for the money. I bet that's it. Maybe she's even given it to you already. . . .'

'Maybe she has and maybe she hasn't.'

There was no one more irritating than Robin in that kind of mood . . . especially when Jessica was planning to ask Granny for money herself. She leaned back against the railings, forgetting the need to keep moving. If Granny *had* given money to Robin, would it strengthen or weaken her case? On the one hand it seemed only fair that if Robin had got something he wanted, she should get something too. But would Granny Knott see it that way? Or would she simply see that the little stash of fivers she kept rolled up in her stocking had almost disappeared?

As she pondered this point, time ran out.

Louise came racing down the path. To Jessica's horror she came straight towards them. There were tears streaming down her face.

'It's gone ... my bracelet's gone,' she sobbed. 'It was nine carat gold and Daddy'll kill me and it wasn't my fault,' she wailed. 'I just asked Mrs Lovett to look after it for me and she went and let it get stolen!'

'Oh no, Louise. That's terrible.' But before Jessica could dart forward to comfort her special friend, Robin had lumbered in between them.

'You could earn a fiver a week cleaning your old man's Porsche, Louise,' he said rudely. 'At that rate you'd soon save enough for a new bracelet—if he doesn't sack you first.'

73

7

A Nasty Suspicion

JESSICA SAT ON the bottom of her grandmother's bunk with her arms round her knees. She had spent the last hour digging potatoes. Now she was back inside supposedly to tell her grandmother how many bags she'd filled and how big the spuds were, but really to see if the right moment had come for her all-important question.

Thoughtfully Jessica looked at the humped figure in the bed. Granny Knott hadn't been her usual busy, bossy self that morning. She'd known exactly what time of day it was—but she'd still decided to go back to bed after breakfast. She wasn't sick, she insisted—just tired and in need of a lie down.

Should she? Shouldn't she? Would she? Yes. She took a deep breath.

'Please will you give me the money for culottes, Granny?' she blurted.

The bedclothes heaved. 'Cool hots? Is that some kind of new-fangled take-away food?' asked Granny Knott hoarsely.

74

In spite of herself Jessica giggled. 'You don't eat them, Gran,' she explained. 'They're something you wear—a cross between shorts and a skirt. They look like a skirt, but the material is sewn up the centre. Like this.' She demonstrated with the front and back of her Oxfam skirt.

Granny Knott's eyelids drooped wearily. 'If you ask me yon's just an excuse for girls til swing about like monkeys without showing their knickers,' she croaked. 'Clothes should look like what they are. . . .'

'But they're Brownie uniform. And I need a pair for my Promise Ceremony. And Mrs Lovett will get me them in Belfast on Monday only I have to give her the money today. Please, Granny, say yes. Please.'

At this the old lady opened one watery deep-set eye and gave her granddaughter a piercing sidelong glance.

'How much do they cost?' she croaked.

'Umm.' This was the tricky bit. Jessica had forgotten to find out the exact price but she knew even the cheapest clothes seemed dear to Granny Knott. 'If you give me a twenty pound note, I'll bring you back loads of change,' she said quickly.

'Twenty pounds!' Both her grandmother's eyes were wide open now and full of indignation. 'In my day you could have bought a full-grown cow for less . . . Twenty pounds indeed!' She broke off, overtaken by a fit of coughing.

Oh dear! Jessica helped her sit up in the bed and fetched her a glass of water. But underneath she felt anything but sympathetic. Why did Granny Knott have to be so mean? Why did she always spoil things?

'Please, Granny,' she pleaded. 'I *really* want them. And you gave Robin the money for his bike.'

'Me! Give him money!' Granny Knott spluttered. 'I did no such thing.'

'You did give him money. You must have. He's gone to pick the bike up this morning, hasn't he? He's got what he wants. And now I want something too.'

'Want . . . want . . . want . . . Is that the only word in your vocabulary?' The old lady lay back on her pillows and shut her eyes. 'Go on then. Go and take what you want from the stocking. But just remember, it was your old worn-out grandmother worked her fingers to the bone til provide for you and your brother both, and all *she* wants is a bit of peace and quiet. . . .'

Leaving her grandmother dozing in the bedroom, Jessica shut the door of the mobile home behind her and made her way down the path. She supposed a true Brownie would have stayed around after getting her twenty pound note and offered to make a cup of tea. But she wanted to get to the church and pay for her culottes as soon as possible.

Or did she? At the gates of the depot she stopped and thought for a moment. Should she go straight to the church? Or should she sit in her tree for a while and try to prepare herself for her next meeting with Louise.

Would they still be best friends? That was the question that continued to haunt her as she scrambled up to her familiar perch and sat there ten feet above the pavement. Would Louise remember how they had sat side by side on kneelers, or would all that closeness have been blotted out by Robin's dreadful outburst at the gate? Jessica gritted her teeth. Then, thankfully, she fingered the folded bank-note in her pocket. If I can just get her talking about Brownies and culottes and Promise Ceremonies again, she thought, everything might be all right. ...

It was a crisp clear autumn morning. The world seemed aglow with colour. In the near distance, Jessica could see the green playing fields of Laganvale College, with their red-roofed pavilion. Further back the spire of St Peter's Church pierced the horizon, silhouetted against a pale gold backdrop of sky. Directly across the road the white walls of Mount Arabis glistened through a framework of russet-brown leaves.

She pondered the mystery of the missing bracelet. What had Louise's dad done when he heard the terrible news? she wondered. Of course everything *looked* as perfect as ever on the other side of the road. But appearances could be deceptive. Mr Witherspoon could at that very moment be ranting and raving beside the swimming-pool.

'Stolen, you say? Your bracelet's been *stolen!*' Jessica imagined him slamming his fist down on a sun-lounger. She frowned. It was very confusing. Things oughtn't to get stolen at a Brownie meeting where everyone was meant to do Good Turns and think of others before themselves. At the same time she knew valuable bracelets didn't hop out of velvet boxes of their own accord. So could Louise herself have taken it out to show someone? And then accidentally lost it?

Jessica looked again at the church spire, letting her mind wander over possibilities. Perhaps she should ask Jesus to show her where the bracelet had gone. After all, he'd helped her in quite a few ways lately. She'd prayed for Louise as a friend—and got her. She'd prayed about culottes—and got them. So why not pray she would find the bracelet? That would really make up for Robin's nasty remark. She could just imagine the look on the other girls' faces when she handed it in. 'Of course I've learned to expect this sort of thing from Jessica,' Mrs Lovett would say thankfully. 'She's one of the brightest, best-dressed Brownies in the Pack.'

A sudden flurry of action on the road

finished that particular daydream. First Mr Witherspoon's Porsche pulled in through the gates. And then an orange-overalled driver got out of a lorry. As Jessica watched he approached Mr Witherspoon.

'Can you spare a minute, boss?' she heard him say.

Side by side the two men disappeared round the back of the office.

The little incident reminded Jessica that she ought to do some more work on her school project. Maybe, with Mr Witherspoon's permission, she could talk to the driver about his latest delivery. And follow this in her project book with a full-page drawing of his wrinkled monkey face.

She scrambled back down to the ground and walked in through the gates of the depot. But as she made her way towards the men, she heard Mr Witherspoon let out a huge angry bellow. Perhaps this wasn't such a good time for research, she decided, stopping in her tracks. Still, she couldn't resist a quick peep down the gap between two lorries to find out what had thrown Louise's dad into such a rage.

She saw him standing beside the driver, pointing at the back wall of the office.

'Get that cleaned up!' he bawled.

She poked her head round a little further and saw the slogan, painted in huge, wobbly red letters: THE THREE HOODS STRIKE AGAIN.

It's that gang, she thought. The vandals who slashed the tyres last week. They really seem to have it in for Mr Witherspoon.

With a sober feeling she slipped back out through the gates.

'Troubles never come singly,' Granny Knott always said. Jessica felt really sorry for the Witherspoons. First the tyres, then Louise's bracelet, now this.

Again she wished there was something she could do to help. But there wasn't time for her to climb back up her tree and dream about it now. She had culottes to pay for. She must head for the church.

She reached St Peter's three quarters of an hour into the annual church sale. The bottom half of the hall was a mass of stalls—white elephant, books and toys, cakes, plants, garden produce—while in the top half people sat round little tables drinking morning coffee.

To begin with Jessica couldn't see Mrs Lovett anywhere. She saw the Rector, perched at a coffee-table like an uneasy ostrich wondering what to do with its legs. Then she spotted Sharon, with her tray of Brownie calendars, sandwiched between the garden produce stall and the white elephants. And finally she saw her Guider, almost completely hidden from view behind the leaves of a magnificent spider plant.

Jessica felt in her pocket for her twenty pound note and pushed her way through the crowd.

'Excuse me, Mrs Lovett. I've come with the money for my culottes.'

Before the Guider could reply, a tall elegant figure bore down upon them, brushing aside an over-enthusiastic assistant who was trying to interest her in a Busy Lizzie.

'Ah, there you are, Mrs Lovett. A quick word, please.'

It was Mrs Witherspoon, clearly in no mood to support the sale.

'Perhaps we should move somewhere more private,' Mrs Lovett gestured towards an empty coffee table in the corner.

'That won't be necessary. The bracelet hasn't turned up, I take it?'

'I'm afraid not,' Mrs Lovett shook her head. 'Of course I'll be investigating. . . .'

'Quite,' interrupted Mrs Witherspoon. 'I just wanted to be sure you undestood what a serious view my husband and I take of this affair. If the theft had taken place in a park or a super-market . . . or in some other public place where one might expect to rub shoulders with the criminal element . . . but to think it happened in a *Brownie* meeting, on *church* premises, under the supervision of the *minister's* wife . . . well, what can one say?'

Jessica's heart went out to her Guider. She looked as if she'd been slapped in the face.

81

'I'm really very sorry, Mrs Witherspoon. I find it very hard to believe that one of the Brownies could have taken it. . . .'

'Well, did you happen to notice any non-Brownie person entering the hall? That scruffy boy, for example, who was hanging about outside when we came out. Where did he come from?'

Where indeed? Jessica clapped her hand to her mouth.

The finger of suspicion was pointing at Robin.

'I felt small enough as it was, behind that spider plant.' Isabel Lovett was back in her own kitchen, shredding cabbage with quick, angry movements. 'The last thing I needed was Mrs Witherspoon telling the whole congregation I couldn't be trusted to run a Brownie Pack.'

'Did she really say that?' her husband asked sympathetically.

The Guider shot him a glare. 'Well no, not in so many words,' she admitted. 'But it amounted to the same thing. I'm pretty sure if I don't get this bracelet business sorted out fast, she's going to stop Louise coming to Brownies.'

'Brilliant!' Sharon looked up from her homework. 'Louise is nothing but a spoilt little trouble-maker. . . .'

'Nobody is ever "nothing but" anything,' the Reverend Lovett murmured.

His wife and daughter exchanged glances across his head.

Mrs Lovett sighed. 'Well, let's just say we're all a mixture of good and bad. But in Louise's case the bad's more obvious.'

'Quick, Jessie! Outside! I've something to show you.' Robin burst through the caravan door and grabbed his sister by the hand. The sullen scowl of the last few days had completely disappeared. He was glowing with happiness and pride.

Jessica could guess even before she stepped out into the garden what she would find.

Yes. There it was. Propped against the wall of the tool shed. Bigger and brighter and better-looking than ever. One gleaming purple and yellow Aztec mountain bike.

'Whoopee!' Robin whooped and sprang on to the saddle. 'Watch this!' He performed an impressive series of loops and spins.

'See you later.' With a triumphant wave of his hand, he free-wheeled down the garden path and turned out on to the open road.

At last he had gone. And Jessica could wipe the false, fixed smile off her face. The evidence was mounting. Up until that moment she had refused to believe it. But now she had no choice.

He had his bike.

Granny Knott insisted she hadn't given him a penny.

Could he have stolen Louise's bracelet and sold it to get the money?

8

A Terrible Shock

LOUISE WASN'T AT school on Monday.

'Please, Miss Forbes, she's sick,' Rosie announced at roll-call.

'How do you know?'

'What's wrong with her?' Rachel and Ruth huddled round her desk at breaktime to discuss the situation.

'I know 'cos I called at the house. Poor Louise! You should have seen her. Her eyes were like two red bulges in her face. Mrs Witherspoon said it was flu—but it looked more like lost-braceletitis to me. She probably spent the whole weekend crying.'

'She was so proud of that bracelet,' Rachel sighed. 'Imagine somebody sneaking over to Mrs Lovett's table and taking it!'

'You'd wonder how anyone could be so mean,' Rosie nodded. 'Mrs Witherspoon told Mum she was going to make an example of the culprit. I wouldn't be suprised if she sends the police round to Brownies next week.'

The police! Jessica had been sitting apart from the rest of the group, pretending not to listen. But now she jerked in her seat, rocking the desk and knocking a felt-tip over the edge on to the floor. Plop.

The sound attracted her classmates' attention. They looked across and nudged each other.

'Where did you disappear off to last Friday then, Beansprout?' called Ruth.

'I felt sick. I ... I was in the church,' stammered Jessica. 'With Louise.'

'That was handy,' said Rosie with a sly smile. 'Anyone would think you knew something was going to happen and arranged to be out of the way. Are you sure you didn't have inside information?'

'Wha ... what do you mean?'

'Mrs Witherspoon told my mum your brother was in the hall at the end of the meeting.'

'I don't know. I didn't see him. He was waiting outside ...' Jessica tried to keep the panic out of her voice.

'He was in the hall,' Rosie repeated firmly. '*And* since Friday he's been riding around on a brand new bike.'

The three Rs exchanged a further round of winks and nudges.

'I don't think it'll take the police long to find their thief,' said Rachel.

'Sounds like they've got a strong suspect already,' said Rosie.

'Mrs Lovett'll be relieved when it turns out not to be a Brownie,' nodded Ruth.

That afternoon Jessica sat in her tree looking across at Mount Arabis through a blur of tears. 'I couldn't help it, Louise,' she found herself whispering. 'Honestly. It was nothing to do with me.' But she didn't expect anyone to believe her. Any day now the police would arrive. Robin could end up in court. Oh the disgrace of it! Two words kept pounding in her brain. Bad blood. She didn't quite know where she'd heard them before, but she knew what they meant. Bad blood was what Robin had in his veins—the sort of blood that made him lie and steal. And because she was his sister they would say she had bad blood too. Culottes or no culottes her friendship with Louise was over . . .

There weren't even cornflakes out for tea when she finally arrived back at the mobile home. Since taking to her bed on Saturday morning, Granny Knott had forgotten about meals. Now she was stretched out on the window seat, with her head propped up against a box of onions, snoring loudly. She'd removed her false teeth, so her mouth had caved in. She wore flannel pyjamas over her dungarees and duffel coat over the pyjamas and a purple mohair cardigan over the coat.

Jessica felt she had never seen such a horrible sight.

As she stood there wondering whether or not to raid the stocking for money for chips, there was a knock at the door.

She froze. Could it be the police in search of Robin?

It turned out to be Sharon with a message from her mum.

'Well, aren't you going to open it?' she demanded when Jessica continued to stand white-faced and shaken in the doorway.

Without any enthusiasm, she took the note out of its envelope.

Dear Jessica, This is just to bring you up to date with what we did in the Beginners' Group on Friday. As you know we are preparing for the Promise Ceremony the week after next. I have asked the group to learn their Brownie Promise off by heart. I hope you will be able to find time to do this, and also to finish off your Brownie Promise Book. See you on Friday. Isabel L.

'If you like I could stay and teach you the Promise now,' offered Sharon.

Jessica moved aside to let her into the van, hoping against hope that she wouldn't notice the snoring rag-bag among the onions.

'I promise that I will do my best, to do my duty to God, to serve the Queen and to keep the Brownie Guide Law,' she muttered. 'I know the words already.'

'Well done,' beamed the Sixer. 'All you've got

to do now is turn up on the night. You *are* going to be there, aren't you?' she continued a little anxiously, when Jessica didn't reply.

'I don't know. . . .'

'The girls in your class have been saying things, haven't they?' Sharon jumped to her own conclusions. 'But listen, you *mustn't* let them put you off. Everything is going to work out. They won't go on saying nasty things much longer. Believe me. I *know*.'

'I've got to make the tea.' Jessica backed towards the cooker. It was all very well for Sharon to be so certain. She was one of the lucky ones. Of course things always worked out for girls like Sharon. . . .

There was no one to work things out for Jessica.

For several minutes after the Sixer left, she sat with her chin cupped in her hands thinking how hopeless it all was.

She had no one to turn to. No mother. No father. For a little while after their conversation in the church she'd thought Jesus might help. She knew better now. Instead of changing her life for the better, he'd made it worse. She had *more* to be ashamed of. More than ever.

She felt another surge of helpless anger. If only she didn't have a family like Granny Knott and Robin, she might stand a chance of doing something for herself. But they were like

Cinderella's two ugly sisters, spoiling things, ruining her chances. Bad blood. Just because she lived under the same roof, everyone would believe she had it too ... unless ... unless. ... Slowly an idea formed in her mind. With a sense of quiet desperation she took a notebook and pencil from her schoolbag.

'Dear Louise,' she wrote. 'I have something to tell you—something I've never told anyone else. ...'

Louise didn't return to school for the rest of the week. Then on Friday she reappeared, rosy-cheeked and radiant, standing with the three Rs at the back of the Brownie Hall.

'You're better!' Delighted, Jessica darted towards the group only to come up against a wall of stony looks.

'I got your letter,' said Louise unsmilingly. 'So. What's the big secret?'

'Can we talk outside? I don't want everyone listening.'

Rachel, Rosie and Ruth moved in a little closer round their friend, as if they feared for her safety.

Louise shrugged. 'I suppose I might as well go with her ... not that it'll make any difference. If I'm not back in ten minutes tell Mrs Lovett.'

At last they were alone together—face to face in the pink-tiled privacy of the ladies' cloakroom.

'Well, what is it?' Louise looked over Jessica's shoulder into the mirror and fluffed out her hair. 'If you're going to tell me your brother took my bracelet, I already know. And if you're going to ask me to stop my parents going to the police, don't bother. The report's already in.'

'Does that mean the police'll search our house?'

'Probably.' Louise nodded sourly.

Jessica bit her lip. This was it. She had her speech ready and this was the moment to make it.

She took a deep breath. 'I'll be glad if they do. Maybe then someone'll discover who I really am.'

'What do you mean, who you really are? You're Jessica Knott.'

'No I'm not. I only found out myself a few weeks ago. I came across this box full of letters and papers in a cupboard . . . written to Granny Knott by some man with a foreign name . . . saying that she would be paid a whole load of money for looking after a baby girl.'

'What!' Louise stopped admiring herself in the mirror. 'You don't mean . . .?'

'That baby was me,' Jessica nodded. 'I knew the minute I started reading. Everything fitted. I saw why I'd never loved Robin and Granny Knott, and why they'd always been so horrid to me. They're not my real family. My real parents aren't Irish at all . . . they're Italian . . . an

Italian count and countess. I was kidnapped the day I was born.'

'Wow!' A thoughtful expression crossed Louise's face. 'We always said you were different. Ruth said it was because you were a dirty gypsy ... but. ...'

'My real parents are rich,' said Jessica quickly. 'They live in a ten-bedroomed villa with a veranda and vines growing up the wall and a whole garden full of orange trees. I saw a picture of it among the papers. But you won't tell, will you? Granny and Robin would kill me if they knew I'd talked. They're so cruel, Louise. Look!' She rolled up her sleeve to reveal a series of scratches where she'd fallen into some brambles gathering blackberries.

Louise was suitably shocked. 'That's terrible. But why don't you just take the letters to the police?'

'They've been burned,' Jessica sighed. 'Granny came in and found me reading them and burned the whole box. No. All I can do is hope my parents find me ...' She held up her wrists. 'Before it's too late.'

'Well? What was all that about?'

'Did Beansprout come clean about the bracelet?'

'We were getting worried. We were just about to call Mrs Lovett.' The three Rs buzzed round like flies the minute they returned to the hall.

Louise swatted them with an airy wave of her hand.

'Her name is Jessica not Beansprout. Now mind your own business. We've things to discuss.'

Oh what a joy to see her tormentors sent, muttering, to their Six corners, while she had Louise all to herself. They had things to discuss ... important things. Louise wanted to know every detail of her life with the Knotts. For the rest of the meeting she was rarely more than an inch away from Jessica's elbow. And Jessica's mouth was rarely more than an inch away from Louise's ear. Whisper ... whisper ... whisper ...

They discussed food.

'Granny Knott piles hers and Robin's plates up high as mountains. Then, when they've both finished, she gives me the scraps,' Jessica explained.

And bedrooms.

'I don't really have one. Granny Knott makes me sleep on a pile of old newspapers on the floor. And when the weather gets cold Robin comes in the middle of the night and steals all my blankets.'

And clothes.

'As soon as I get home Granny makes me take off my shoes and Robin hides them, so I have to walk around in my bare feet.'

And colds.

'No matter how ill I am she makes me work at the vegetables, but if he gives even a little cough she fusses round like he's dying.'

The blacker Robin and Granny Knott were painted, the better Louise seemed to like it. Her expression became more and more like that of a Persian kitten fed with dainty morsels of fish. Meanwhile in the background, Mrs Lovett became more and more exasperated.

'Girls, will you *please* pay attention,' she said in the end. 'You've chattered your way through prayers, and through the Pow-Wow and through the games. I don't know what you have to discuss that's so interesting . . . but we're about to get into our Challenge Groups, so let's have a little concentration.'

'Excuse me, Mrs Lovett, are those our culottes in that white plastic bag on the table?' countered Louise. 'Can Jessica and I go out to the cloakroom to try them on?'

Five minutes later, as a result of this brainwave, they were alone again, arm in arm in front of the full-length mirror.

'How do we look?' Louise did a little twirl.

With her head on one side, Jessica studied their reflections. She was reminded of two chocolates—a creamy white one (Louise) and a small dark one (herself), both with milk chocolate bottoms. Only, thanks to the painstaking accuracy of Mrs Lovett's measurements, her bottom fitted more neatly than Louise's.

'Good enough to eat,' she said.

In a different way, Louise saw the same thing. 'I think so too. We really set each other off . . . like strawberries and cream. . . .'

94

Her smile faded and she clutched Jessica sympathetically. 'I suppose you've never tasted strawberries.'

Jessica mentally dismissed the rows of strawberry plants behind the mobile home, loaded with fruit each summer. She shook her head.

Louise tightened her grip. 'I tell you what. I'll get Mum to invite you to my house for some proper food ... steak and baked potatoes and pineapple cheesecake. If you like you can stay for a whole weekend. That way you'll get to sleep in a proper bedroom, with a TV and a video. And Mary will bring you breakfast in bed on Saturday morning. What do you say?'

'Yes. Oh yes, please,' Jessica gasped.

'That's settled then.' Louise unzipped her culottes. 'Then when your parents come, you can invite me back to Italy for the weekend. And we can go in a gondola and eat spaghetti bolognese. . . .'

It was as if the bracelet had never come between them. No ... this was even *better* than before.

Jessica hated to mention it—to run the risk of spoiling things— but she had to be sure. . . .

'You really understand about Robin, don't you?'

'Course. No worries.' Louise pulled on her primrose track-suit and fluffed out her hair. 'If he wants to be a criminal and get himself arrested that's his business. It's nothing to do with you.'

This time when they came back into the Brownie Hall, the three Rs were hopping up and down beside the door, their eyes popping with excitement.

'Guess what? They're here!'

'With Mrs Lovett.'

'In the church.'

Jessica's heart skipped a beat.

'Who's here?' demanded Louise.

'The police, silly. They arrived just after you went into the ladies. Look, you can see the car through the window.'

Sure enough, outside in the carpark, in the gathering dusk, Jessica could make out the shape of a white car with a thimble-shaped bump on its roof.

'They're coming to take you away. Ha! ha!' chanted Rosie.

And with that Mrs Lovett's head appeared round the doorframe. 'Jessica. Come here, dear.'

Louise instantly sprang between them. 'Leave her alone. You can't hand Jessica over to the police just because Robin took my bracelet! It isn't *her* fault.'

For a second the Guider looked mystified . . . then angry. 'Your bracelet is the last thing on anyone's mind right now, Louise . . . the very last thing,' her voice shook slightly and she swallowed. 'Now please, girls. Go into your Challenge Group and look over your Promise. Jessica, you come along with me.'

She had finished her instructions in her usual calm tone. But it fooled nobody. She was upset. They could see it. They had heard the tell-tale quiver.

'Something's happened,' Rosie whispered, as the four very subdued Brownies made their way to their seats and got out their Brownie Handbooks.

The time for messing was over. Something had happened. And that something—whatever it was—must be serious.

The church was dim and ghostly. Mrs Lovett held aside the blue velvet door-curtain, and Jessica stepped through, catching her breath as if she had stepped into cold water. She was shivering. And frightened. There were two police officers waiting silently beside the pulpit— a man and a woman.

'This is Jessica,' Mrs Lovett's voice broke the silence.

The woman officer stepped forward. 'Hello, dear.' She took Jessica's hand and sat down beside her in the front pew. Mrs Lovett positioned herself on the other side with her arm round the girl's shoulder.

'What is it?' Jessica whispered. 'Tell me. What's wrong?'

The policewoman looked into her eyes. Kindly. Sympathetically.

'You're going to have to be very brave.'

Jessica bit her lip and stiffened.

'Your brother and your grandmother are in hospital. . . .'

98

9

In the Kitchen

'HELLO. IS THAT Laganvale Primary school?
May I speak to the headmistress please? Mrs
Benson? Oh good! I'm sorry for disturbing you.
My name is Lovett—Isabel Lovett. Yes, that's
right. Sharon's mother.

'I'm telephoning about one of your pupils—
Jessica Knott. You heard about the accident,
did you? Shocking ... yes ... absolutely. ...
The police think the grandmother had a stroke
and that her brother was knocked off his bike
going for help. Of course they can't be sure
until they've talked to him. No. He's still
unconscious. Old Mrs Knott seems a bit better
today though.

'That's one of the reasons I was ringing
actually. Ralph, my husband, is taking Jessica to
the hospital this morning, so obviously she
won't be at school. She's staying with us. Not at
all. We're delighted to have her—poor child.
She was at Brownies when the news came and
it seemed the obvious thing.

'How is she coping? Well, it's hard to say. Still very shocked, of course. And withdrawn. You wouldn't know what was going on in her head. She hasn't wanted to go anywhere so far. That's why we're so pleased she's agreed to see her grandmother ... although of course it won't be easy.

'Yes ... certainly ... I'll tell her that. She's actually quite keen to get back to school ... tomorrow probably ... or maybe even this afternoon if she's up to it. That's right. Best to keep life as normal as possible until we see how things go. I mean, with strokes and head injuries, you never really know, do you?

'Yes, of course, I'll ring immediately if there's any change in her brother's condition. But the doctor warned it could be several days before he comes round ... and after that ... well, yes ... I'm afraid that's really all we can do. ...'

Bluebell ward—where Granny Knott had been taken—smelled of hard boiled eggs and floor mops.

The nurse led Jessica and the Reverend Lovett to the third bed on the right. 'Here we are.' She whipped around a set of curtains and Jessica found herself sitting in an armchair by her grandmother's side.

It was a moment before she could bring herself to look at the figure in the bed. And when she did look, for another moment, she thought there'd been some mistake. Could this be Granny Knott? This tiny wisp of a woman with a bare pink scalp showing through her hair. Jessica couldn't remember the last time she'd seen her grandmother without a hat. Granny Knott believed in hats. She had a man's peaked cap for wearing outside and a felt beret for inside and a striped nightcap for bed. 'If the National Health warned folks proper about the evils of draughts til the head,' she always said, 'they could close half the sick beds in the country.'

The dungarees had gone too. And the duffel coat, mohair cardigan and flannel pyjamas.

Jessica stared. And gulped. This stripped, hatless, mini-version of Granny Knott wasn't even snoring. Just lying there with her eyes tight shut . . . .as if she couldn't bear to see how the National Health had treated her.

'There. We're feeling *much* better this morning, aren't we dear?' The nurse lifted one spindly wrist from the bedspread and checked Granny Knott's pulse. 'Go on. Say hello, lovey.' She turned to Jessica. 'Your granny might not look as if she's listening. Like the Sister explained, she isn't able to speak or move much at the moment. But your voice is just what she wants to hear.'

How did she know? Jessica wondered. How could this nurse possibly know what Granny Knott wanted if Granny Knott wasn't able to tell her?

'Go on, Jessie,' the Reverend Lovett encouraged.

'Hello, Gran. It's Monday today. Monday morning. Are you awake?'

The figure in the bed moved slightly. One hand plucked at the faded yellow bedspread. And Granny Knott's eyes opened.

'There!' beamed the nurse. 'What did I tell you! She's delighted to see you. Now you set her mind at rest. Tell her how happy and well-looked after you are.'

'I'm staying with the Lovetts, Gran. In the big rectory. Across the road from the church. I'm not giving any trouble.'

Granny Knott's hand plucked faster. She opened her mouth. 'Argh..' she spluttered. 'Argha ... ar ... ar ...'

'Hold her hand and give her a little kiss,' said the nurse.

Jessica looked away from the bed ... down to the other end of the ward, where a huge colour television set sat up on a ledge in the corner, showing cartoons which no one was watching. Wham! A cartoon mouse hit a cartoon cat over the head with a cricket bat ... and a huge lump sprang up on the cat's head.

'Ar ... argha ...' spluttered Granny Knott. Her voice was higher and louder. 'Raghra ... Raghra ...'

'Quick, dear. One little kiss. Then you'd better go.' The nurse smoothed the bedclothes and the Reverend Lovett caught hold of Granny Knott's hand.

'No. You don't understand.' Jessica blinked and backed away from the bed. 'It isn't a kiss from me she wants. She's asking for Robin.'

Robin had been taken to a much bigger hospital in Belfast.

'We could take a race over now and see him if you like,' the Reverend Lovett suggested as they got into the car. 'He's still unconscious, but he'll know that you're there.'

Jessica promptly burst into tears.

She was still rubbing her eyes and sobbing when they arrived back in the rectory kitchen, where Mrs Lovett was up to her elbows in Christmas cakes.

'What do you mean upsetting the poor child like that?' she scolded.

Then she shooed her husband into his study and gave Jessica the job of washing the dried fruit, because, she said, they might as well keep all the waterworks in the same part of the kitchen.

'Somehow I've got landed with the job of baking cakes for half the family,' she went on as Jessica sniffed and hiccuped over the sink. 'There's my two sisters and Ralph's aunt. When I even hint they might like to make their own for a change, you'd think I was suggesting they should climb Mount Everest ... Here. Leave that.' She set a plate of gingerbread and a glass of home-made lemonade on the table. 'Don't you worry about going anywhere. You're staying right here with me.'

The rectory kitchen was wonderfully warm and homely. One half of the floor was tiled and the other half carpeted. If she stayed, Jessica knew Mrs Lovett would let her stretch out in front of the electric fire on the carpeted half and scrape Christmas cake mixture from mixing bowls.

She thought of Robin—all bandaged up and surrounded by machines, in his high white hospital bed.

'Please, I'd rather go back to school.' She pushed away the glass. 'I already missed a whole week's work when I was sick. I don't want to get more behind.'

Everyone at school was very kind. Miss Forbes didn't knock on Jessica's desk. The three Rs didn't call her Beansprout. And some of the boys from Robin's school stopped her on the way home to ask how he was.

At lunch-time she would sit with all the other girls and open the packed lunch Mrs Lovett had made her up that morning. There would be fruit and yoghurt and six sandwiches wrapped in cling-film. And then at the very bottom of the box she would find a surprise. One day it was a home-baked biscuit, with her name and three kisses iced on top. Another day it was a tiny teddy bear with a placard saying: 'Hug me!'

On Wednesday it was a packet of heart-shaped sweets.

Jessica hadn't felt hungry since the accident. So every day she dumped her lunch in the playground rubbish bin when no one was looking. But she kept the surprises wrapped up in a paper tissue in her pencil case. And from time to time during lessons, she would unwrap the tissue and take a look, just to check that they were still there.

At lunch-time on Wednesday, after one last long look, she scraped the icing off the biscuit and handed the whole lot over to Louise.

'You haven't told anyone, have you?' she whispered. 'You haven't told anyone the things I said?'

Louise opened the love-hearts and stuffed six in her mouth at once.

'Course not. When the three Rs were blabbing on about how terrible the accident was, I just told them they'd better be really nice to you or one day they'd be sorry.'

Thoughtfully she sucked and chewed.

'I guessed you'd rather tell them yourself.'

'That's right.' Jessica bit her lip. 'I mean everything's different now.'

'Isn't it just!' Louise tucked into the biscuit. 'You must be over the moon ... living with the Lovetts ... free of Granny Knott and Robin at long last.' She squeezed Jessica's hand. 'I've asked Mummy to invite you for tea tomorrow before the Promise Ceremony. That way we can spend time together ... although I suppose now you're living with the Lovetts, I'll have to invite Sharon too.'

'I'm making my Brownie Promise tomorrow,' Jessica told her grandmother at visiting-time. 'It's a very important ceremony. I have to say the words in front of the whole Pack.'

'That's marvellous!' cried the nurse. She bent down and shouted into Granny Knott's ear. 'Did you hear that, dear? Your granddaughter's going to make her Brownie Promise. . . . There, look! She's opened her eyes. She's really pleased.'

'I'll be a proper Brownie then, Granny. And Mrs Lovett will give me my Promise Badge.'

Granny Knott plucked the bedspread. If she was pleased, she had a very funny way of showing it. 'Arg . . . Raghra . . .' she moaned, tossing her head from side to side on the pillow. 'Raghra ... Raghra ... Raghra ...'

That evening Jessica sat by the electric fire in the rectory kitchen with her Promise Badge Book. She still had one page left to fill in ... the one where she was supposed to draw pictures of herself ... doing her duty to God.

She lay back against the legs of Mrs Lovett's armchair, wishing she hadn't left this particular page to the end. It gave her a horrible feeling inside. These days when she thought about God (and she tried to do as little of that as possible) she pictured a fierce angry giant of a man ... twice as big as Mr Witherspoon, with a beard six times as long ... smashing his huge heavy cudgel down on Robin's head.

Her chin wobbled.

Sharon looked across at her. 'What's the matter? Are you stuck?'

'I can't ... think ... of anything to draw ...' Jessica sniffed.

Sharon made the sort of suggestions you'd expect: going to church ... reading the Bible ... saying her prayers.

The Lovetts were all on friendly terms with God. They said grace before meals and had family prayers at night. Jessica always sat through these times with her fists clenched, especially when the Reverend Lovett asked God to make Granny Knott and Robin better soon. He didn't understand. God wouldn't let Robin get better ... he was too busy punishing Jessica for what she'd done. 'Granny makes me sleep on the floor,' she'd said. 'Robin beats me up. He's so cruel.' It hadn't been true. Not a word.

'Do you know what Louise drew on that page?' Mrs Lovett called over from the sink. 'She drew herself sitting on a swing. And when I asked how that could possibly be her duty to God, she told me it showed her not killing, stealing or telling lies.'

The Reverend Lovett started to laugh, but Sharon flushed red with annoyance: 'Well . . . *honestly* . . .' she said. 'I hope you said she should add "not being nasty to people" to her list.'

'Personally I don't go in for all these "nots",' said her dad. 'If I was becoming a Brownie'—he wrapped the tea-towel round his waist to represent Brownie culottes and saluted—'I wouldn't "not" be doing anything . . . I'd be letting God do all sorts of things for me . . . forgive me, love me, cheer me up.'

'So how's Jessica meant to draw that?' demanded Sharon.

'All Jessica needs to draw,' her father removed the tea-towel, 'is a cross.'

Jessica felt a wave of relief. That was easy. She could draw a cross without even thinking.

But somehow she couldn't help thinking as she drew. Could the Reverend Lovett be right? Could God be so much nicer than she thought?

On the other side of the room the telephone rang.

Sharon grabbed her mother's arm. 'Help! It's Mrs Witherspoon. She said she'd ring after tea to see if you'd let Jessica and me go round to Louise's tomorrow. Please! Don't make me! Say no!'

'Don't be silly, Sharon.' Mrs Lovett shook herself free, but her husband had already lifted the receiver.

'Yes . . . speaking . . . oh really . . . yes, that *is* good news . . . certainly it would be a pleasure . . . I'll ask her right away. . . .'

Sharon rolled her eyes.

But the message wasn't from Mrs Witherspoon. It was the hospital.

'Jessica!' The Reverend Lovett reached for his minister's collar and started fastening it into place. 'Robin's woken up, and he's asking for you. Are you ready to come with me now?'

It was very late when Jessica finally went to bed that night. She'd spent an hour sitting with Robin in the hospital, and another hour with the Reverend Lovett in the car and then another hour with Mrs Lovett in the kitchen. After all that talking, Mrs Lovett had said she was starving so she'd dished up sausages and chips.

They'd tasted great.

'We won't worry about school tomorrow. Ralph'll ring Mrs Benson and explain.' She popped her head round Jessica's bedroom door to say a last goodnight.

'Goodnight, Auntie Isabel. Goodnight, Uncle Ralph.'

With a sleepy smile, Jessica snuggled down deep into the mattress.

It felt funny in a really nice sort of way, calling them by their Christian names for the first time.

10

In the Jacuzzi

THE WONDERFUL SENSE of relief was still with her when she woke up next morning. Granny Knott's stroke and Robin's accident hadn't been her fault. She wasn't to blame. The Lovetts had been absolutely clear about that.

'OK so you thought your life would be easier if you didn't have a grandmother like Granny Knott and a brother like Robin,' Uncle Ralph had said. 'Lots of us have those sorts of feelings about family members. It doesn't mean we really want to get rid of them. And it certainly doesn't mean that anything bad that happens to them is our fault.'

'Of course God wouldn't want you to tell made-up stories about yourself,' Auntie Isabel had smiled. 'But he isn't going to punish you for it—that would just make you feel worse about yourself than ever.'

She had reminded Jessica of one of the stories they'd talked about in prayers—the story of Zacchaeus.

Jessica read it for herself in the children's Bible that morning before getting out of bed. Zacchaeus had been small, just like her. And very unpopular. As a tax-collector he'd collected a lot more taxes from people—even poor people—than they were supposed to pay. 'I daresay he was ashamed and didn't like himself much,' Auntie Isabel had said, and Jessica could see why. But the interesting thing was that Jesus had taken a different view. Out of all the hundreds of people who had lined the road to watch him coming into town, Jesus had chosen to walk alongside Zacchaeus all the way back to his house for tea.

Amazingly Jesus hadn't wanted to punish the little man, Jessica noted; he'd wanted to be his friend. And she noticed something else as well. Afterwards Zacchaeus had gone round all the people he'd stolen money from and paid it all back.

She got up then. She still felt better—much better. But before she could look her reflection straight in the face again, there was something she had to do. She was going to Louise's for tea that afternoon. Some time between four o'clock when she was due to arrive and twenty-past six when she would leave for her Brownie Promise Ceremony, she had to tell Louise the truth.

'Ah, Jessica. How lovely! And Mrs Lovett, how kind! But no Sharon. A pain in her stomach!

111

How dreadful! Louise ... Louise ... come quickly, dear. It's Jessica.' Mrs Witherspoon flapped and cooed like a beautiful dove when she opened the door.

'Jessica ... Jessica ...' Louise burst through from the kitchen corridor and danced across the marble hallway to throw her arms round her friend. 'I was telling Mary what we wanted for tea. I didn't hear the car.'

'Louise is so fond of Jessica,' Mrs Witherspoon cooed, pecking the top of her daughter's head with her lips.

'Of course. We all are.' Mrs Lovett gave a little wave. 'Bye, pet. Have a nice time. I'll see you both later at Brownies.'

If it hadn't been for the shadow of confession-time looming ahead, this visit would have been a dream come true. Louise waltzed Jessica straight upstairs to her bedroom.

It was the beautiful, exciting, fairy-tale room Jessica had always imagined. The walls were palest rose pink, with a border of curtsying ballerinas in floating white dresses. The carpet was pink too and patterned with white roses. There were fitted wardrobes. And a white TV set. And a pink wash-hand basin. And an archway leading through into an Aladdin's cave full of treasures.

Louise, it seemed, possessed every toy that had ever been advertised. She had an army of Sindy and Barbie dolls. She had a typewriter and a tape recorder and a video camera and a computer. She had a completely furnished playhouse. She had cupboards stacked full of books and games.

Most marvellous of all—she had a suitcase full of clothes for dressing up. 'Is this the way your mother dresses when she goes out at night?' breathed Jessica, wrapping a silver-grey fur over a strapless black evening frock and then holding up her skirt to admire her high-heeled sandals.

'Only if it's a dinner dance,' Louise emerged out of the other end of a filmy nightie. 'If it's bridge she wears slacks and sweaters. She won a fruit cake in a tournament last week, and her outfit cost so much Daddy said he'd paid five pounds for every currant.'

'Gosh!' Jessica held up a marigold-coloured jumper, with three velvet bumble-bees buzzing across the front, wondering how many currants it was worth. It was like studying life on another planet. A thought struck her: Robin and Granny Knott must have seemed as fascinating and fantastic to Louise as the Witherspoons seemed to her now. The only difference—the girl sighed and kicked off her fairy-tale slippers—was that Louise's stories about her family were true.

Hanging her head, she flopped down beside the open suitcase on the carpet. 'Louise,' she said in a small voice, keeping her eyes fixed on a single white rosebud, 'I've something to tell you.'

Before she could get any further, Louise had grabbed her hand.

'No! Wait!' she cried. 'I've something to tell you too, but we can't talk here. Let's go and soak in the jacuzzi. I'll ring down for Mary to bring us milk-shakes.'

The jaccuzi was a round turquoise pool in the centre of the Witherspoons' bathroom in which warm water bubbled and frothed out of eight jets round the side. Sitting in it, wearing one of Louise's bikinis and sipping chocolate milk-shake seemed to Jessica the absolute peak of bliss. Not even the thought of being sent straight back to the rectory in disgrace could stop her delighting in the stream of water gushing out against the small of her back.

'Oh Louise,' she sighed and sipped. 'I could sit here for ever.'

'Could you?' Louise set down her glass with a business-like air. 'Could you really? Does that mean you wouldn't let anyone stop you coming to visit . . . as long as I wanted you to come?'

What a crazy question. 'Of course I wouldn't!' Jessica gulped.

'Good!' Louise actually sounded relieved. 'That's what I wanted to talk to you about. There's been a bit of a problem, you see.'

'What sort of a problem?'

'It's Daddy. He was in one of his moods last

night. When he heard me telling Mummy to invite you here, he got really mad and shouted and told her to do no such thing. Of course Mummy didn't listen to him. I'd already explained that you were my best friend and I needed you to stay here with me whenever I wanted. She just went ahead and rang Mrs Lovett anyway.'

Jessica felt as if the milk-shake in her stomach was turning sour.

'He . . . he didn't want me to come. But why?'

'You've never heard such a stupid reason. Dad sacked Robin because he suspected he was part of some gang who go round vandalising property and stealing things. Then the Saturday I was sick, they painted their name—The Three Hoods—in white paint over his Porsche.'

The Three Hoods. Jessica remembered the slogan on the office wall. And she remembered something else as well: Robin vowing to get his own back on Withers. Could he? Would he?

'But Robin can't be part of the gang. He's in hospital,' she tried to sound casual—as if she didn't really care.

'That's just it. Since his accident, nothing more has happened. That's why Dad's more convinced than ever that Robin's the ringleader. He's said so to the police.'

Jessica immediately imagined two police officers striding into Robin's hospital room.

Making his injured head pound with their questions. It was a hundred times worse than she'd thought: stealing a bracelet was one thing. Robin might just get off with a warning for that, especially if he seemed truly sorry and promised to sell his bike and give Louise the money. But being a member—maybe even the ringleader—of a gang like The Three Hoods was much more serious. People—even children— got locked up for that sort of behaviour. 'Raghra ... Raghra ... Raghra ...' Granny Knott would moan. But Robin wouldn't come. Not for months and months. He'd be in a detention centre.

Louise was looking at her anxiously. 'We mustn't let it come between us.'

'No. No, we mustn't,' Jessica echoed.

'So remember—if there's another row over tea—we're best friends and Mummy's on our side and Daddy isn't half as fierce as he sounds.' Louise stood up and grabbed two thick lavender bathtowels from the heated towel-rail. 'You ignore him. That's what Mummy and I always do.' She handed a towel to Jessica. 'Here. We'd better get dressed. What was the thing you had to tell me?'

Jessica sat shivering on the edge of the jacuzzi watching it froth and bubble round her feet. 'Um ... I've forgotten ... nothing important ... I'll probably think of it later,' she said.

The meal was served by Mary in the sun-lounge. Jessica sat on one side of a long glass table and Louise on the other. Mrs Witherspoon, who was going out for dinner later, helped herself to fingers of toast from the trolley.

Louise clearly intended to make her Brownie Promise on a full stomach. She selected a double portion of chicken Kiev from Mary's serving platter, surrounded it with roast potatoes, rashers of bacon, and pineapple rings, and then drowned the whole lot in tomato ketchup.

'Watch you don't get a stain on your uniform, darling.' Mrs Witherspoon flicked a crumb from her skirt.

'You're like me, Jessica,' she observed, as Jessica cut her own chicken into smaller and smaller pieces on the plate without ever raising her fork to her mouth. 'I can never manage much before an important event. I remember the last time I went to Hillsborough to meet His Royal Highness, all I could bear to nibble was a sliver of kumquat.'

Jessica wasn't listening. She had just heard Mr Witherspoon's voice in the hallway. Her mouth had gone dry.

'Hello . . . hello . . . hello . . .' He came in rubbing his large red hands together and sniffing. 'Something smells good. Full plate, Princess.' He pinched Louise's cheek. But no sooner did he spot Jessica, than all his good humour disappeared.

'What's this?' he bellowed at his wife. 'Who have we here?'

'It's Jessica, Reginald. Jessica Knott. Louise's little friend from school.'

'Little friend from school, indeed.' Mr Witherspoon glared. 'I thought I had made myself clear last night. She's no suitable friend for Louise.'

'But I *like* her,' Louise wailed. 'And you don't understand . . .'

'I understand all right. Oh yes, I understand. What I understand is that my wife and daughter go out of their way to defy me . . . without the slightest regard to the problems I'm facing at work. Didn't you listen to one word I said last night about that . . . that . . . delinquent brother of hers?'

'But Robin isn't her brother,' Louise shouted.

'And Speedy Transport may rule *your* life. But it doesn't rule *mine*,' said her mother.

Jessica rose to her feet. She was reminded of her first Brownie Good Turn . . . of her meeting with Mr Witherspoon . . . of the way she'd had to think fast and speak out. Now, for Robin's sake, she must do it again. She must try to convince Louise's dad her brother *wasn't* guilty. She must throw the police off his trail.

'Please, Mr Witherspoon,' she cried. 'Please, you've made a mistake. You ought to know what Robin's like. He's not the sort of boy to go round slashing tyres and throwing paint in the middle of the night. He's far too dreamy. And as for being a ringleader, why he couldn't lead anybody anywhere. I mean he can't even arrange the vegetables on Granny's stall properly. All he ever wants to do is listen to music and eat chips and ride around Laganvale on his bicycle. . . .'

'A bicycle purchased under *highly* suspicious circumstances . . .'

'If you're talking about Louise's bracelet being stolen . . .' Now Jessica's tongue had loosened it just kept going, as if it had a mind of its own. 'Robin had nothing to do with that. It was me. I was jealous, you see. I hated living in a caravan and being teased by the girls at school. I wanted money to make things different.'

'*You* took Louise's bracelet?' said Mrs Witherspoon faintly.

'You wanted *money*?' Mr Witherspoon choked.

'Oh . . . Oh . . .' Louise's face was the same colour as the ketchup. 'Oh, Jessica. How *could* you?'

'I don't know.' Jessica looked at her, straightening her shoulders, relieved in spite of everything that she had found some way of making it up to her brother for the things she'd said. 'I'm really sorry. All those things I told you about Robin and Granny. They were lies. All lies. Robin's the nicest brother any girl could have. And Granny always tried her best to look after us. I miss them so much. I really do. . . .'

She turned on her heel and fled from the room.

11

In the Transport Lorry

MARY WAS ON her way into the sun-lounge with a tray of knickerbocker glories.

Jessica almost knocked her over as she ran. 'Please could you open the front door for me? I've got to go.'

In the background she could hear Mr and Mrs Witherspoon and Louise still arguing and shouting at the tops of their voices.

'Had enough of them, have you?' Mary steadied herself and abandoned her tray on top of the grand piano. 'There be times when I feel the same myself. Come on then.'

Clunk. A welcome rush of cool air hit Jessica's face as the front door of Mount Arabis shut behind her. She took a deep breath, then continued her flight down the drive, her sense of relief growing with every step. Her only fear was that the Witherspoons would come after her. She didn't know how she would answer their questions. They would want to know what she'd done with the bracelet. They might ask how she'd managed to be in the church talking and in the Brownie Hall stealing it at the same time.

One thing was certain. She couldn't go on to the Brownie meeting now. She would have to hide somewhere until it was over and then slip back to the rectory when the coast was clear. Perhaps by that time she would have thought up a good enough story to convince everyone that she, and not Robin, had been the thief.

On reaching the bottom of the drive, she paused. Where next? Her tree? No. It was so bare of leaves at this time of year, she might as well try to hide in a goldfish bowl. The mobile home? No. That was too obvious. The Witherspoons were bound to look there.

It had started to drizzle. Grey clouds hung over the distant hills making the late afternoon dark. Through the gloom Jessica's eyes were drawn to one brilliant splash of colour—the line of orange lorries in the depot. She ran across the road, through the gates, past the office, and down the side of the line.

Just as the drizzle turned to rain, she found what she'd been hoping for. A lorry with its rear doors open a crack. Jessica didn't waste any time. Within seconds she had disappeared from view . . . into the back of a Speedy Transport van.

It seemed a suitable place to consider all that had happened over the last two days. Tugging the doors shut behind her without completely excluding the light, she stood for a moment, taking stock of her surroundings. Four bare walls. A couple of large packing cases. And a pile of sacking in the corner.

She was able to make herself cosy. She lined a packing case with sacking, climbed in and pulled some more sacking round her, like a mouse burrowing into its nest.

She had a question to ask herself. Why was it that in spite of the complete breakdown of her friendship with Louise she didn't feel too miserable? She was confused, yes. She didn't know whether trying to take the blame for the missing bracelet had been the right thing to do or not. That was why she'd needed to get away. To find somewhere private to think it over. But miserable? No, quite the opposite. Rather to her surprise, Jessica realised that she felt happier than she had done for a very long time.

I suppose Zacchaeus felt really happy too after he'd paid back the people he'd taken money from, she thought.

But there was more to it than that. This wasn't just the thank-goodness-that's-over kind of happiness you felt after a visit to the dentist. It was something much deeper. A quiet, contented feeling that from now on things would be better. Zacchaeus had been able to hold his head up and make a new start because he had Jesus for a special friend. And at that moment curled up in her packing case, Jessica felt she could do the same. From now on it wouldn't matter so much that her family was different from other people's; or that she didn't live in a proper house; or that most of her clothes came from the Oxfam shop; that her hair was dark, not fair and her arms were thin, not chubby. Uncle Ralph had said that Jesus loved her just the way she was. And somehow she had been able to believe it ... to understand the way Zacchaeus felt ... called out of his tree to meet the most important person in the whole world who amazingly thought he was someone important too.

Of course there was still the question of Robin.

But there too the weight had lifted. It was as if her outburst in her brother's defence had helped her to see him in a new light. She found herself remembering all the nice things about Robin: the way he had been so kind to her when she was sick; the way he fed the birds outside the mobile home in the morning; the way he wrote poems in a jotter and kept them hidden under his mattress. She had set out to deal with Mr Witherspoon's suspicions, and had ended up dealing with her own.

She leaned back, feeling the scratchy warmth of the sacking all around her.

'I don't believe Robin would slash tyres or throw paint round the place, Jesus,' she murmured. (It seemed the most natural thing in the world to talk to her new friend.) 'I don't even believe he took Louise's bracelet. I mean he isn't all that good—but he isn't that bad either. So do you think . . . I was just wondering . . . is there some way you could help him to make a new start too?'

Outside the rain continued to fall. Chin up . . . chin up . . . chin up . . . Was it her imagination or did she hear a whispered message of encouragement in the gently beating rhythm? This was the moment when normally she would have drifted off into her daydream world. But she didn't need to be rescued by imaginary parents any more—not now she had someone a hundred times more powerful than any Italian Count to look after her. Chin up . . . chin up . . . chin up, the rain seemed to say. Her eyes grew heavy. She would shut them. Just for a moment, she thought. . . .

She drifted. Floating through time. Dreaming a delightfully happy dream which somehow managed to include Robin and Jesus and Zacchaeus and Mr Witherspoon. And then, suddenly, she was awake again. As wide awake as anyone would be if they had just been hit by a blast of cold air.

The rear doors of the lorry had been flung open.

'In here! Quick!' A boy's voice hissed.

'Give us a hand up,' a second boy panted.

Jessica lay absolutely motionless in her sacking nest, scarcely daring to breathe. What was going on?

The whispering continued.

'Phew! That was close!'

'You said it. The squad car must've been just down the road.'

'D'you think they spotted us?'

'Nah. You got the money?'

She heard the rustling sound of a plastic bag being opened and the faint click of a torch being switched on.

A small bubble of light appeared on the side of the packing case just above her head. Cautiously Jessica lifted a finger only to discover a round hole no bigger than a cherry.

'It's here. All notes,' the first boy was hissing. 'The guy at the till handed it over just the way Big Mac said he would. It was easy as eating doughnuts.'

'Sixty ... eighty ... one hundred ... ten ... twenty ... thirty. Wow! We've just walked out of Witherspoon's Service Station with a cool one hundred and thirty smackers!'

'I wouldn't say cool. They're hot. Real hot.' The boy with the bag gave a nervous laugh.

'Yeah, well, we'll just lie low here till the coast is clear. And then head for the call-box.'

More cautiously still Jessica lifted her head. And, yes, she could see out. What's more her spy hole was in exactly the right position to allow her to study the speakers. There they were, crouched on the floor of the van, their figures illuminated by the light of a torch—two teenagers in anoraks with hoods so large they completely obscured their faces.

Heart pounding Jessica sank back into her sacking. Of all things—she had ended up under the same roof as two of The Three Hoods.

Up until that moment if she had thought of the gang at all, she had pictured them as the sort of shadowy, sinister characters who somehow vanished into thin air when their evil deeds were done. But now she could see for herself how human they were. They didn't even sound spectacularly wicked.

Once more she raised her eye to the spy-hole, squinting curiously. The Hoods had moved back to lean against the side of the van, shoulder to shoulder. They were discussing the raid. The one with the nervous laugh was afraid he'd spotted a video camera on the wall of the service station. He was afraid the police might be able to recognise them from a tape. He was wondering if they ought to dump their anoraks . . . in case they could be identified.

Serves them right if they are, Jessica thought. If it hadn't been for them and all the trouble they've caused, Robin wouldn't have lost his job.

In the distance a siren sounded, filling the air with a vibrant, piercing wail.

'The police!' one of the lads gasped. 'They must have seen us after all . . . Ed, we're done for . . .'

'Nah. They'll never look here.'

'Yes they will.'

'OK then. What d'ye want to do? Run for it?'

'Too late. What about those packing cases? We could hide in there.'

'Good thinking! C'mon then.'

Oh no! Jessica froze.

It all happened in a matter of seconds. First she felt the case rock. Then came a crushing weight on her shoulder.

'Ow! Get your foot off me,' she screamed. 'This was my hiding-place first!'

12

Explanations

'HELLO, MRS LOVETT? ... Marcia Witherspoon speaking ... your husband is still out searching for that wretched child, I take it ... what? ... he's just returned ... and? ... no sign of her ... well, *really* ... if I could get my hands on the little madam I wouldn't be held accountable for my actions ... to go missing ... on a night like this ... dragging people's husbands out into the middle of a downpour to hunt the streets ... upsetting everyone's plans ... I must say, I thought at the time it was unwise to take a child from that sort of background into your home. I can understand you may have felt it was your duty ... what's that? ... where else could she have gone? ... well, how should I know? ... I'm not a social worker ... I'm merely suggesting that it might have been wiser to let the professionals handle things ... the child is obviously disturbed ... I mean, one can't believe a word she says, can one? ... If you'd *heard* the stories she told Louise! ... and then to disappear like that ... upsetting our entire household ... Reginald and I were supposed to be going out to dinner tonight ... yes, Mrs Lovett it *is* a shame ... and as if that wasn't bad enough there's been trouble at the service station ... that wretched gang again ... two of them marched in bold as brass and walked off with the contents of the till ... Mrs Lovett ... Mrs Lovett are you still there? ... Good heavens, my dear woman, there's no need to *cry* ... they can't have got more than a couple of hundred pounds and Reginald has the whole incident on video ... oh, you're worried about *Jessica* ... yes, I realise she's been missing for over five hours ... isn't that why I rang you in the first place? ... we're *all* worried ... but one can't afford to give way to one's emotions ... as Reginald says, those sort of children are street-wise ... they know how to survive ... I daresay she'll make her way back to your doorstep well before breakfast. And if you take my advice, you'll hand her straight over to the social worker ... although of course, we would be most grateful if you could first ascertain what exactly she did with Louise's bracelet and whether she was involved in the raid ... Mrs Lovett ... Mrs Lovett ... well *really* ... such *manners* ... she's hung up!'

'Calm down, Gary. And keep your hair on. It's only Robbie Knott's kid sister.'

Jessica sat in the full glare of the torchlight blinking upwards. Over the edge of the packing case hung two identical faces—snub-nosed, wide-mouthed. Recognition dawned. They were Ed and Gary Lyons. She had often seen them in the street—the twins from Robin's form at school. Every now and then Robin had come home grinning over some prank they had played on an unwary student teacher. But tonight there wasn't a trace of mischief on their cheeky, freckled faces. Beneath their hoods they were scowling fiercely.

'Just what do you think you're doing lurking in a packing case like this, spying on us, then half-scaring us out of our wits?' demanded Gary.

Jessica stood up. 'I wasn't spying. I . . . I was hiding from Mr Witherspoon,' she quavered.

'Hiding from Mr Witherspoon, eh?' A slightly more sympathetic note crept into Gary's voice. 'So what are we supposed to do with you now? I mean you've spied on us. You could get us into a load of trouble.'

'You're in a load of trouble already,' Jessica couldn't resist pointing out. 'You can't expect to get away with this, you know.' She nodded over at the crumpled money-bag in Ed's hand.

The brothers exchanged angry, worried glances.

'Look,' said Ed. 'Maybe we can do a deal. I guarantee that once you understand what this is about, you won't want to sneak on us. I mean by the sound of things you can't be that keen on Withers yourself.'

'I'm not keen on stealing either,' muttered Jessica.

'No. Well, neither are we as a general rule. OK we've stolen some money, but it isn't for ourselves. You've heard of Robin Hood and his Merry Men, haven't you? Robbing the rich to help the poor. Well, that's the sort of thing we're involved in.'

Jessica frowned. 'I don't see how slashing tyres and throwing paint on Mr Witherspoon's Porsche is going to help anyone,' she shrugged. 'My brother lost his job because of you—because Withers thought he was part of your stupid gang.'

'Did he really? That's bad!' The freckled-faced twins seemed genuinely concerned. 'Look, how about if we get Big Mac to fix that one? The last thing any of us would want is to get your Robbie into trouble. He's a good sort is Robbie. Minds his own business. Never gets up anyone's nose. It's just . . . when you're trying to sort out someone like Witherspoon . . . well . . . sometimes the good guys get caught in the crossfire.'

Jessica folded her arms and leaned back against her packing case. The siren had stopped. The rain had eased to a gentle patter.

'You're not making a lot of sense,' she said.

Ed and Gary were clearly used to functioning as a twosome. They even adopted a duet approach to explanations. Sometimes one of them started a sentence and the other completed it. Sometimes they said exactly the same thing in chorus.

'It started in September,' began Gary.

'The Board of Governors gave up the idea of a leisure centre for senior pupils,' continued Ed.

'The Head said they couldn't afford it.'

'But Big Mac discovered that wasn't the reason at all.'

'One of the Governors had opposed the scheme. Three guesses who ...'

'Reginald Witherspoon.'

'Said he didn't believe in pampering sixth-formers.'

'Said the leisure centre was a waste of money.'

'Of course he's such a big shot, the Head and the other Governors just let him walk all over them.'

'The seniors, especially the sixth-formers, were really sick when they heard.'

'But nobody seemed to be doing anything about it ... not even a petition.'

'And that was when Big Mac got going. And started The Three Hoods. Aim one ...'

'To let Withers know he couldn't have it all his own way ...'

'Aim two ...'

'To get funds to equip the leisure centre ourselves.'

'And up till now everything's worked like magic.'

'Big Mac reckons we're really hitting his Uncle Reggie where it hurts . . .'

'His Uncle Reggie?' For the first time since the beginning of this saga, Jessica interrupted.

'Oops.' The twins exchanged glances. 'Didn't mean to let that one slip. But if you haven't guessed already, you might as well know . . .'

'Big Mac is Withers' nephew. Which reminds us . . .' Ed tightened his grip on the plastic bag. 'We're supposed to hand this little lot over to him tonight. The question is . . .'

'Will you keep your mouth shut?'

'Now you know what The Three Hoods stand for.'

'You wouldn't want to land us in it, would you? Big Mac would have us for breakfast if he knew we'd messed up. . . .'

Again the girl interrupted. 'Is he that tough?'

'Believe us. You don't want to get on the wrong side of Big Mac Witherspoon,' Gary said earnestly.

'So you won't sneak, will you Jessica? It isn't *wrong* what we're doing—getting senior pupils their rights.'

'And it's already after midnight and we can't let you go until you promise to keep your mouth shut. So come on. What do you say?'

Back in the rectory kitchen Mrs Lovett removed a batch of scones from the oven. 'I'm just terrified something's happened to her,' she remarked over her shoulder. 'Oh Ralph! The child's been gone for over six hours. . . .'

The kitchen door opened. The minister's wife put her finger to her lips. 'As I was saying, I've had the oven on for almost six hours. Oh hello there, Sharon. Can't you sleep either?' She pointed to a mountain of bread and biscuits on the table. 'What would you say to a nice hot scone and a cup of cocoa?'

'I don't want anything.' Sharon sounded as flat and woebegone as a punctured football. 'Did Jessica . . . has Jessica?'

'Got in touch? No. Not yet. But we're expecting her to turn up any minute safe and sound. In the meantime we're just racking our brains to think of places she might have gone.'

Sharon didn't appear to be listening. She held her right hand up over the table and opened her fist. Clink. Something fell down onto the formica surface and lay there—a small golden mound of dainty links.

'It's all my fault,' she said and burst into tears.

'But that's Louise's bracelet!' her mother gasped. 'Sharon, where did you find it?'

'On the table in the Brownie hall,' Sharon wailed.

Mrs Lovett sat down. She looked at the bracelet. She looked back at her daughter. She made a little fluttering movement with her tiny hands.

'You mean you *took* it? But ... but ... you don't even *like* jewellery.'

'I didn't take it because I liked it. I took it to teach Louise Witherspoon a lesson. I only meant to keep it a day or two. But then you said if the bracelet didn't turn up, Mrs Witherspoon would stop her coming to Brownies. So I held on. It just seemed such a brilliant chance to get rid of Louise. I mean we both knew how she was messing things up for Jessica. . . .'

'Stop, Sharon, stop . . .' Mrs Lovett put her hands over her ears. 'I can't believe I'm hearing this! Oh Ralph, what are we to do?'

There was a lengthy pause during which Sharon sobbed quietly, and the Reverend Lovett retreated to the other side of the biscuit mountain to drum his fingers on the back of a chair.

'We can't sit here all night,' his wife said faintly. 'I think perhaps . . . yes . . . that's it. . . .' Her voice gathered strength. 'We must go straight over to Witherspoons with the bracelet. We will explain what happened. You will apologise to Louise, Sharon, and I shall do the same to her mother.' She swallowed. 'If the worst comes to the worst I shall tell her I'm prepared to hand in my Guider's warrant. Because naturally I am as much to blame as you in this affair.'

'No. Don't say that, Mum. It isn't true.' Sharon flung her arms round her mother.

'Yes it is.' Mrs Lovett swallowed again, clearly on the verge of tears herself. 'I knew you disliked Louise. But I let you carry on as if disliking Louise was all part of helping Jessica. Perhaps I even felt that way myself. And this is the result.'

She disentangled herself from Sharon, lifted a banana loaf from the table and reached for an anorak hanging over the back of a nearby chair. 'You don't need to say anything, Ralph. I know what you're thinking. One wrong attitude can poison a hundred right actions.'

Her husband smiled. 'Actually I was thinking it was rather late to call on the Witherspoons,' he said gently. 'I vote we sleep on it, then ring them tomorrow—first thing.'

13

Big Mac

'I CAN'T PROMISE not to say anything about this,' said Jessica. 'Brownies promise to help other people and serve the Queen, not to keep their mouths shut about stealing.

'And don't try telling me what you're doing is OK,' she went on. 'You're fooling yourselves. Even if Mr Witherspoon was the meanest man on earth, it still wouldn't be right to slash his tyres and steal from him.

'And anyway, why should you do Big Mac's dirty work? He may think he's Robin Hood, but he sounds more like the Sheriff of Nottingham to me. Robin Hood didn't sit at home with his feet up waiting for his Merry Men to come back with money.'

Whew! Jessica sat back. Her tongue had done it again. Come out with a whole long speech almost of its own accord. Inwardly she felt as amazed as Ed and Gary looked.

She braced herself, waiting for their shock to become anger. Waiting for them to turn nasty and yell back. But they didn't.

Instead they screwed up their faces sheepishly and scratched their heads.

'Well ... did he?' she demanded, pressing home her advantage. 'If you ask me Big Mac is as mean as his uncle and a lot more cowardly.'

'He didn't join in the tyre slashing or slogan painting. He was afraid he would be recognised,' said Gary slowly.

'There you are, then.'

The twins looked uncomfortable. 'It was part of the deal,' said Ed. 'He caught us skiving in town one afternoon, when we should have been in class. . . .'

'So he gave us the choice. Either be reported to the Head, or help him get his knife into Withers.'

'We didn't want to be reported . . .'

'So we did what we were told. I mean we weren't that fussed about the leisure centre. It was going to be for the senior pupils, anyway. We wouldn't even have been able to use it. But Big Mac had us cornered.'

'That's blackmail,' pronounced Jessica. She frowned, thinking back over her own experience. She knew better than anyone how easily one thing led to another—how without meaning to, you could end up behaving like the sort of person you never wanted to be.

She could see that was how it had happened to Gary and Ed.

Any trace of bravado had disappeared from

their voices. 'Mum will really hit the roof when she finds out about this.' Gary pushed the money-bag away with his toe.

'I see it all now,' muttered Ed. 'We get expelled. Meanwhile Big Mac goes on to become head boy.' He buried his head in his hands. 'He's really used us. The worst of it is, we haven't a shred of evidence to prove he was involved.'

And that was when Jessica—still drawing on past experience—came up with her plan.

Rain bounced off the pavement, gathering in glinting, choppy puddles round the call-box.

'We're meeting him in the pavilion in ten minutes.' The twins rejoined her in the shelter of her oak tree.

'How come you were able to ring without his parents answering? Has Big Mac got a phone in his bedroom?' she asked.

'Nah. His people are away on business. He always picks the nights they're out of town for Three Hood meetings,' shrugged Ed.

'And what about your family?'

'There's just Mum,' said Gary grimly. 'And we stuffed the beds before leaving.'

The girl thought longingly of her own bed in the rectory. They had only just vacated the transport lorry and already she was soaked to the skin. But at least nobody was out walking the dog on a night like this. They had the sodden, black world to themselves.

Within minutes they were squelching across the playing fields of Laganvale College towards the pavilion. It was a squat red-brick building, set between the rugby pitch and the tennis courts. From her treetop vantage point Jessica had often watched pupils spill out of it for matches. She had imagined herself tripping out among them, sporting the green and gold school colours, cheered on by admiring spectators.

The last thing she would ever have imagined was that she should arrive outside the pavilion door at two o'clock in the morning with one hundred and thirty pounds of stolen money in a plastic bag, in the company of two woebegone thieves.

Gary inserted a key into the lock.

Creaking alarmingly the door swung open, and they stepped through into the narrow tiled corridor.

It reaked of damp towels and sweaty feet. In the dim torchlight Jessica took in the layout of the building. A front door—through which they had just entered—leading onto the playing fields. A back door, leading out to the tennis courts. Girls' changing room and showers on one side. Boys' changing room and showers on the other. She wiped a limp straggle of hair off her nose and took a deep breath. So far so good.

Gary, meanwhile, had made his way to a

cupboard at the end of the corridor. 'We're in luck,' he hissed. 'There's paper. Loads of it. Looks like a hundred years of fixture lists.'

'Mac's coming. I can see a torchlight in the middle of the playing field,' Ed called from the door.

Jessica felt the palms of her hands grow sticky. Big Mac was on his way. Was she mad ... imagining she could ever help the twins to outwit him ... a boy over twice her age, over twice her size? Chin up ... chin up ... chin up. In those few brief seconds she found herself remembering another Bible story. The story of David and Goliath. David had defeated the giant because he trusted God.

'He expects to meet us in here.' Ed led the way into the boys' changing room.

'You know what you're meant to do—and what to say at the end?' she asked him anxiously.

'"Here comes the caretaker. Quick. Out through the back." I just hope it works,' Ed added doubtfully.

'It *will* work. Trust me,' said Jessica, on the strength of David and Goliath.

She stepped behind a shower curtain.

'Can you see anything?'

'No,' the twins chorused.

There was just time to watch a spider scuttle down the waste-pipe. Then the whole damp, cheesy atmosphere became electrically charged as Big Mac strode through the door.

'Hold the pickle.' He trumpeted the password as he came.

At the sound of his voice, Jessica went weak at the knees. She was instantly reminded of Mr Witherspoon. But there were differences. Big Mac sounded as polished as his uncle was earthy. Where Mr Witherspoon bristled, Big Mac seemed as smooth as a snake. The girl shivered. For a moment, listening to his sardonic tones, she wished she'd promised to keep her mouth shut after all; gone home when she had the chance. Gary and Ed were well-meaning— but weak. They could so easily be dragged back under their leader's bullying spell. What if they betrayed her? What if, instead of going through with the plan, they whipped back the curtain. Chin up . . . Chin up. I'm like David—trusting God, she reminded herself.

Perhaps it was coincidence but the twins seemed to gain confidence after that.

Their voices sounded less thin and reedy. Ed actually managed to make himself heard above the rustle of notes and the murmur of their leader's self-congratulatory speech.

'The lousy thing is, Mac—nobody's ever going to know the truth,' he said.

'My dear Edward,' replied Big Mac, with exaggerated patience, as if he'd just been addressed by a muddle-headed insect. 'That's the whole point. You don't imagine for one minute that The Three Hoods could achieve their objectives if beloved Uncle Reginald *knew* who was stripping him of his assets?'

'Oh I didn't mean *him*,' said Ed quickly. 'I meant the sixth-formers. The ones who'll be using the leisure centre when we finally get it. Future generations, if you like. Seems a pity they'll never know what they owe to us.'

'Right,' Gary joined in. 'We were just discussing it before you came, Mac. You know the time capsule idea, where people bury stuff to show their descendants what life was like in the twentieth century. Well, we were just wondering if we could make some sort of record of The Three Hoods. To be sealed and buried under the floorboards in the leisure centre.'

Jessica held her breath.

'Hmmm. A memorandum for future generations. The idea appeals,' the polished voice said slowly.

Hurrah! The girl could have hugged the shower fittings. She had been right. Mr Witherspoon and his nephew had something else in common—neither could resist an invitation to boast about their achievements. . . .

She heard the rustle of paper.

'Gareth, are you capable of transcribing my immortal words?' Big Mac enquired.

There followed fifteen minutes of dictation. For the benefit of future generations, Mac related the history of The Three Hoods, taking full credit for everything from start to finish.

'And so remember, college-crested comrades,' he concluded. 'Remember, as you lean upon your snooker cues and turn up the volume on the stereo system; remember that there was a time when, thanks to the petty-minded carping of a mean-spirited millionaire, sixth-formers were in danger of being deprived of such well-earned privileges. Be thankful that Big Mac Witherspoon was willing to fight for your rights. Hold to his vision. Follow in his footsteps. Honour his memory.' He paused dramatically, then murmured. 'I don't really think it's necessary to include any other names.'

'Whatever you say, Mac,' came the deferential chorus.

'Right. Pass it over and I'll sign.'

He had taken the bait—hook, line and sinker. Jessica ought to have been ecstatic, but instead she was in agony. Clutching her tummy . . . pinching her nose . . . sinking down into the corner above the waste-pipe.

'He-he-he-he.' The giggle escaped.

'What was that?' The sixth-former sprang to his feet.

Fortunately Ed proved equal to the occasion. With the speed of lightning he flew to the door, looked out and delivered the line he had rehearsed. 'Here comes the caretaker. Quick! Out through the back!'

Big Mac didn't keep his head. He didn't stop to think the approach of a caretaker across a rugby pitch was scarcely likely to echo in the shower.

Abandoning money-bag and memorandum, he made for the door. And fled.

'I thought the world of that boy.' All eyes were upon Mr Witherspoon sitting, wrinkle-suited and sorrowful, in the middle of the rectory kitchen.

He had brought Jessica home. Never would she forget her welcome—Uncle Ralph's bear hug, the tears of joy streaming down Auntie Isabel's face. Only Sharon had held back—red-faced, puffy-eyed.

'She has something to tell you, Reg,' Uncle Ralph had said.

What could it be? Jessica had wondered and was wondering still. They'd been sitting in the kitchen for the last ten minutes. For the last ten minutes Sharon had looked like a water-logged rain-cloud ready to burst. But she couldn't get a word in edgewise.

Ever since Jessica had presented Mr Witherspoon with Big Mac's memorandum, he'd been babbling on like a bewildered child.

'Thought the world of him,' he muttered again.

'Would you like a top-up?' Mrs Lovett, automatically sympathetic, tilted the teapot over his mug.

'Birthday presents, Christmas presents—you

name it, he got it. I thought he would take over the company. Yes. That was the plan. Often talked to him about it. Told him the pitfalls. Thought he understood. Thought he respected me. But no.'

'Another scone?' murmured Mrs Lovett with a meaningful glance at her husband.

'Petty-minded. Mean-spirited. Carping. You've seen for yourself, Vicar. Those were his words.'

Mr Lovett pushed the memorandum back across the table.

'All very upsetting, Reg,' he agreed, nodding over at Sharon. 'And I'm afraid we're about to add to your headaches.'

Ah! At last. Despite her exhaustion, Jessica straightened in her seat as the older girl made her way to the visitor's side.

'Please will you give this bracelet back to Louise. I took it. I know it was wrong.' Sharon bit a trembling lower lip. 'I'm very sorry.' She dropped the jewellery into Mr Witherspoon's palm.

There was silence. The sort of tense silence you hear in classrooms before exam results are read out. A curious expression appeared on Mr Witherspoon's face. He opened his palm and looked at the bracelet. Then at the memorandum. Then back at Sharon. Then across the table at her dad.

'I really have nothing to add. Except that my wife and I are extremely sorry too,' the Reverend Lovett sighed.

At which Mr Witherspoon smiled—a pale, ghostly, quarter-moon of a smile. 'Would you believe—I'm relieved. Somehow it helps knowing this sort of thing can happen to a vicar.' He shrugged and pocketed the bracelet. 'The kid's apologised. As far as I'm concerned there's nothing more to be said.'

BIG MAC

14

Promise Ceremony

'AND TO THINK I once had a quiet, shy little
sister, who would hardly go into the sweet shop
and ask for an ice-lolly,' grinned Robin, as
Jessica appeared in the ward. 'What's all this
I've been hearing from Sharon about you
unmasking The Three Hoods?'

'Nothing much. I just sort of bumped into
two of them—Ed and Gary. And they sort of
decided they wanted to give themselves up.
And then we had to find some way of making
Big Mac take his share of the blame. And we all
got soaked and I caught a cold. So Auntie
Isabel made me stay in bed yesterday, but I'm
fine today.' Jessica hopped up on his bed.
'That's all.'

'That's all,' mimicked Robin. He lay back
against his pillows with his hands behind his
head. 'I want to hear the *whole* story—blow by
blow. You can take as long as you like,' he
added generously. 'I'm not going anywhere.'

So she told him. She sat up on the bed with

her legs crossed and her hands cupping her chin and relived the whole adventure, from the moment that she first heard Ed and Gary's voices in the back of the lorry.

As she reached the climax Robin let out his breath in a whistle of admiration. 'Phew! Good for you. If ever anyone deserved unmasking, it's Big Mac Witherspoon. He's bullied half the pupils in the school.'

'Well, he'll think twice before bullying anyone from now on,' declared Jessica. 'As soon as he'd run off through the back door, Ed and Gary and I went straight out of the other door and round to Mount Arabis with the money. We told Withers exactly what had been going on. Of course he was really mad and didn't believe us at first. He thought you had to be the third member of the gang. He nearly blew his top when we said it was Big Mac. Then when we gave him the confession, he was like a pricked balloon. Told Ed and Gary to go home and he would decide what he was going to do later.'

'And what *is* he going to do?'

Jessica shrugged. 'Send Big Mac to a psychologist for a start. He thinks the pressure of studying for exams has unbalanced his brain.'

'*Him! Studying!* That's rich!' hooted Robin.

'Well, it's a big problem,' Jessica murmured. 'What do you do when someone you love very much breaks the law and you don't want them to be punished?'

'Eh?' her brother stared.

She reddened. 'That was what Uncle Ralph said—when Withers went home. He said Withers felt about Big Mac the way he felt about Sharon and the way I felt about you and the way God felt about all the people in the whole world. That's why he sent Jesus.' She stopped.

'Sounds like Withers might do better skipping the psychologist and sending Big Mac for a session with you in the rectory!' grinned Robin. 'Speaking of which, Sharon had some long involved tale about Louise's bracelet, only I was so flummoxed by what she'd told me about you, I didn't listen properly. What's the story there?'

'Um . . .' Jessica hesitated. She had been hoping he wouldn't ask about that. 'There was a bit of a mix-up. I thought *you'd* taken the bracelet, and Louise thought *I'd* taken the bracelet, but all the time it was Sharon. We've got everything straightened out between us now, though.'

'Hang on a minute. Did I hear you right? You thought *I'd* stolen Louise Witherspoon's bracelet!'

Jessica hung her head. 'I'm really sorry. It was just the way things happened—her bracelet going missing at exactly the same time as you got the money for the bike.'

'Well thank you very much.' Robin folded his arms. 'Didn't it ever occur to you that Granny had given me the money?'

'She told me she hadn't.'

'So?' Robin shrugged. 'You know Granny. . . .'

Their whole mood sobered. 'Poor Granny!' A tear rolled down Jessica's cheek: the helpless bareheaded old lady in Laganvale nursing home seemed so far removed from the bossy, bustling granny they had known.

'How is she?' Robin muttered.

'Um . . . OK. Sitting up in a chair. But she doesn't speak. The first few times I went in I thought she was trying to say your name. But she doesn't even do that now.'

He sighed. 'I wasn't going to tell you this, but I suppose . . . I mean, you seem so much braver somehow . . . Granny isn't fit to look after us any more. A social worker came to see me yesterday to discuss what was going to happen when I got out of hospital. I told her I wanted us all to go back to the mobile home. But she said that wouldn't be allowed. She asked me how I would feel about being fostered.'

'Fostered? You mean, being part of somebody else's family? Would I be fostered too?' said Jessica. 'Would we be fostered together?'

'That's the idea . . . although the social worker says it isn't so easy to get families for boys my age. Eight-year-old girls are less trouble. . . . So the only way we could be together to begin with might be in some sort of orphanage. A group home, the social worker called it.'

'Oh!' said Jessica. Another tear rolled down her cheek at the thought of leaving the Lovetts.

Robin reached out and took her hand. 'Don't worry, Jessie. I'll look after you.'

They were still sitting holding hands when the Lovetts arrived to pick her up.

'How do you feel today, Robin?' Ralph Lovett pulled two chairs up to the bed. 'At least you're nice and warm in here. It's freezing outside.' He helped his wife take off her coat before sitting down.

Jessica's eyes widened in surprise. 'I thought you wanted to go into Guide Headquarters for badges, Auntie Isabel.'

'Er yes, that was the original plan.' Mrs Lovett looked apologetic. 'But my problem—you've probably noticed this—is that once I get an idea in my head, I find it terribly hard to wait. I just couldn't concentrate on badges. I'd probably have bought all the wrong ones. I mean Ralph thinks it's too soon to say anything, but I feel we have to mention it, to give you both time to think things over . . . and decide what you want to do.'

Jessica knew then—she was talking about the future. She wanted to know what their plans were.

'You needn't worry,' she said quickly. 'We've already decided. We're going to give the group home a try.'

'You are? . . . Oh, well, I suppose there's

nothing more to be said . . . if that's what you would prefer. . . .' The Guider's voice had gone flat.

'What we would *prefer* is to back in our own place,' growled Robin. 'That's the only way Granny will get better. It's no wonder she isn't talking where she is at the moment. Probably the only vegetables she ever sets eyes on are in her soup.'

'And if we can't go home we would prefer fostering,' added Jessica. 'Only we don't think that would work either because we want to be together.'

'But . . . but . . . of *course* you'd be together.'

Jessica shook her head. 'The social worker says it's very hard to find families for two— especially when one of them is a boy like Robin.'

'In that case . . .' The Reverend Lovett cleared his throat, and Jessica saw that his face had lit up in one of his rare smiles. 'I happen to know a couple who feel that a girl like you and a boy like Robin would just make their family complete.'

'It's such a big rectory . . . with so many spare bedrooms . . . and cooking for five would be so much more economic than cooking for three . . . and, well, the thing is . . . we really *want* you . . . both of you . . . for as long as you care to stay.'

'You mean *you* want to foster us? Why, that's *brilliant!*' Jessica bounced up and down on the bed.

'You don't need to decide anything right away, Robin,' Ralph Lovett observed quietly. 'You can let us know in your own time.'

The boy frowned. Jessica stared at him anxiously.

'I can let you know now,' he said gruffly. 'You've seen for yourselves how Jessie feels about it. Of course it's different for me ... I'm older. I don't need anyone looking after me or telling me what to do. But I suppose, for her sake, if you're *sure* it isn't going to be too much hassle—I'm willing to give it a try.'

'So now you and Robin are staying at the Lovetts'. And I've got my bracelet back. And Daddy is happy for us to be best friends. And tonight we're going to be making our Brownie Promise ... Oh Jessica,' Louise clasped her friend's arm as they walked down the path towards the Brownie Hall. 'Isn't everything wonderful? I'm so glad Rosie and Rachel were sick last week and the ceremony had to be put off. I was really disappointed at the time. I mean you *know* how long it took me getting ready. But I'm glad now, because it means we're making it together, just the way we'd planned.'

'There's one thing a bit different.' Jessica moved slightly ahead and stood in the circle of light around the main door. She unzipped her coat. 'I had to borrow an old pair of sweat pants from Sharon. My culottes got ruined in the rain last week.'

'Oh no!' Louise's face fell. 'That means we won't be the same after all.'

'Never mind. We'll be saying the same words.'

'I suppose so.' Louise cheered up. 'Mummy says I have to remember to speak out clearly so that I can be heard at the back of the hall. I bet Ruth's mummy won't hear *her*, even if she's sitting in the front row. Ruth's the worst ever mumbler. Sometimes you'd think she had her mouth full of marbles.'

'It's the braces on her teeth.'

'Well wouldn't you think her mummy would tell her to take them out before the ceremony, then?'

'Not really.' Jessica smiled. 'I think it's OK to mumble as long as you mean what you say. Come on.' She pulled Louise's arm. 'Let's go inside.'

At long last the moment had come. Jessica stood in the centre of the Brownie Ring, with the other Beginners. It would be her turn next. In a few seconds she would be making her Brownie Guide Promise.

The Brownie Hall was full for the occasion. Two rows of parents and relatives were sitting under the platform. Jessica felt a sudden pang. The other new Brownies all had someone of their own to hear them. Up until that moment she had been hoping that Uncle Ralph would turn up in time to listen to her, but he must have got delayed.

'Now Jessica, are you ready?'

Here we go. She nodded solemnly at Auntie Isabel.

'Do you know the Brownie Guide Law?' Mrs Lovett asked.

She took a deep breath.

'A Brownie thinks of others before herself and does a Good Turn every day.'

'Do you know that if you make the Promise, you must always do your best to keep it and carry it out everywhere, but especially at home?' asked Mrs Lovett.

'Yes,' Jessica replied.

'Will you make your Promise as a Brownie Guide?'

As Jessica raised her hand in the Guide salute, there was an unexpected interruption. The door into the Brownie Hall swung open behind her. She saw Auntie Isabel's face light up and the Brownies on either side staring. She looked round. Then squealed with surprise. Uncle Ralph hadn't been delayed at a committee meeting after all. He'd been driving round in his car—first to the hospital and then to the nursing home. He'd collected Robin and Granny Knott!

There was a buzz of conversation as the little group clattered up the side of the hall towards the platform. Granny Knott was in a wheelchair, but from somewhere the nurse had managed to dig out her old raincoat and workman's cap. Robin was walking beside her. He had grown even taller during his stay in hospital. Jessica could see three inches of tartan sock beneath the bottom of his jeans.

She caught her breath, hugging herself with delight. *Her* granny. *Her* brother. Here to hear *her*.

Mrs Lovett started to speak again.

She said how wonderful it was that Granny Knott and Robin could be there to hear Jessica make her Promise. She said that Brownies had to work hard to keep their Promise in all sorts of little ways every day, but that from time to time they might be called upon to keep it in a big way. She said that that was the sort of special challenge Jessica had faced the previous week. And she had handled it wonderfully—with great ingenuity and presence of mind.

'Now Jessica,' she finished. 'Your granny and your brother have made a special effort to be here so we mustn't disappoint them. Let's take the ceremony all over again, right from the beginning. Do you know the Brownie Guide Law?'

Somehow Jessica managed to control her excitement long enough to stammer out the right answer. She was embarrassed. She was thrilled. She felt like laughing and crying both at once.

But by the time they reached the final question she was ready to do justice to the words she had learned and thought about so carefully.

'Will you make your Promise as a Brownie Guide?' Mrs Lovett asked.

'I promise that I will do my best: to do my duty to God, to serve the Queen and help other people and to keep the Brownie Guide Law,' Jessica replied steady and clear as a bell.

Most Guiders had to bend over to pin badges onto T-shirts, but Auntie Isabel was small enough to take one step forward and do the job standing straight.

'I trust you to keep the Promise,' she said.

There was a brief hush. Then clap . . . clap . . . Mr Witherspoon started it, Mrs Witherspoon joined in, and suddenly everyone was clapping their hands and cheering—all the other Brownies, all the parents. . . .

For a moment Jessica looked startled. What was going on?

Chin up. Chin up. Chin up.

The penny dropped. This was for her too!

Chin high, she left the Ring. She skipped the full length of the hall. The applause rang out louder than ever, and she stood, straight and smiling, between her brother and the wheelchair before bending down to put her arm round her grandmother's shoulders.

'Isn't it great? I'm a Brownie now, Granny!'

As her ear drew level with Granny Knott's mouth, tears of joyful amazement sprang to her eyes. Her grandmother was clapping. But that wasn't all.

'Jess-ica ... Jess-ica ... Jess-ica ...'

The old lady was cheering too.

Tracy And The Warriors

by Lynda Neilands

Tracy is a nine-year-old Brownie, and she is homesick. Sent to stay with her grim aunt and wild cousin, she pours out all her woes in letters to God.

Her cousin and his friends (a gang of so-called warriors) lose no time in making life difficult for Tracy, but she finds help from the visiting Circus. When the warriors burn down Carlo the clown's caravan, all seems lost. Is it possible for anything good to come out of such a disaster?

LYNDA NEILANDS is the writer of *The Brownie Handbook*. She lives with her family in Dublin, in the Republic of Ireland.

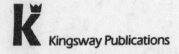

Kingsway Publications